A Short Life
Well Lived

A Short Life
Well Lived

A NOVEL

Tom Sullivan

HOWARD BOOKS
A Division of Simon & Schuster, Inc.
New York Nashville London Toronto Sydney

Howard Books
A Division of Simon & Schuster, Inc.
1230 Avenue of the Americas
New York, NY 10020

First Howard Books trade paperback edition June 2011

HOWARD and colophon are trademarks of Simon & Schuster, Inc.

For information about special discounts for bulk purchases, please contact Simon & Schuster Special Sales at 1-866-506-1949 or *business@simonandschuster.com*.

The Simon & Schuster Speakers Bureau can bring authors to your live event. For more information or to book an event contact the Simon & Schuster Speakers Bureau at 1-866-248-3049 or visit our website at *www.simonspeakers.com*.

Designed by Davina Mock-Maniscalco

Manufactured in the United States of America

10 9 8 7 6 5 4 3 2 1

Library of Congress Cataloging-in-Publication Data

Sullivan, Tom.
A short life well lived : a novel / Tom Sullivan.
p. cm.
1. Blind—Fiction.   2. Attorneys—Fiction.   3. Sick children—Fiction.
4. Cancer—Patients—Fiction.   5. Boston (Mass.)—Fiction.
6. Domestic fiction.   I. Title.
PS3569.U35925S36 2011
2011002119
813'.54—dc22

ISBN 978-1-4391-9227-6
ISBN 978-1-4391-9579-6 (ebook)

*To Molly Newberry and all the children
who taught me the true definition of courage
as they fought to overcome cancer
in all of its anguish and in all of its forms.*

acknowledgments

To Dr. Glen Komatsu: You started me on the road to understanding the complexity of palliative care.

To Dr. Pamelyn Close: This work could not have ever been written without your talent, heart, time, and remarkable knowledge in the understanding and treatment of pediatric cancer.

To my sister, Peggy McVarish: Your battle with this dreaded disease made the writing of this book very personal to me and brought complete focus to my work.

To my agent, Jan Miller: I'll keep writing them; you keep selling them. As always, thank you.

To Jennifer Stair: When you're editing my work, I'm never afraid to walk the plank because I know that you're always there to catch me.

To Julie Cremeans: So this is our fifth book together. Your friendship, love, commitment, and talent always give me the confidence to be the best writer I can be. Thank you, thank you.

To Rev. Clayton Cobb: It's almost impossible to express how much your friendship means to me, but that friendship has now been enhanced with a spiritual awareness that had not been a part of my life. With your help, heaven might just be in my future.

prologue

I've heard it said that life is a marathon—a race to the finish twenty-six miles and three hundred and eighty-five yards long. Our mile markers are the years—five, ten, twenty, fifty, seventy-five—and the finish line is death . . . or is that just the starting line? Is the marathon of our lives only the beginning of eternity? Who can know? And what if you're forced, due to injury or illness, to drop out of the race early, to end the competition long before expected?

I'm Brian O'Connor, a husband, a father, a lawyer, and a man who happens to be blind. On this pristine Monday in April, I stand in Hopkinton, a small suburb of Boston, at the start of the Boston Marathon. Thousands and thousands of people's lives will be changed forever as they snake their way to downtown Boston. The first twelve miles are downhill, and then they will face Heartbreak Hill, which is actually five hills, as they struggle to reach the top and hear the cheers from the coeds of Wellesley College.

So on to Boston, and then what? Glory? I run the race with my guide and friend, the Rev. Clayton McRae. He's been my spiritual mentor, but today he's just a guy trying to keep me from tripping on the thousands of feet that will pound the streets. We've drawn a spectacular morning. The temperature, which can range in any given year from seventy degrees down to below freezing, is about fifty and perfect for running, so we won't have to pay the price of either frostbite or heat exhaustion.

The bands are playing. The flags are waving. The crowd of athletes and nonathletes is pressed together, edging toward the starting line, bodies compressed into a sea of humanity, nervous at the challenge before them but hopeful in their attempt to complete this life-changing journey.

I am in my late thirties. I'm fit and I have trained to be here, and the man running next to me is committed that we will cross the line in Boston together in a very respectable time of three hours and thirty minutes. That means we'll run a pace of about eight minutes a mile—three hours and twenty-eight minutes, to be exact.

I sense the bodies move. We are starting. Somewhere in the middle of the pack Clayton and I are walking, trying not to trip. We are at least a quarter of a mile from the starting line when the bodies begin to move, so we are not yet running. We are not yet official until we cross the line. We are not yet on the clock.

To be Tommy's father, to be married to Bridgette, and to have a daughter like Shannon, is to be complete. As I move, carried by the crowd, toward that point when time will matter, I'm remembering when it did not.

chapter 1

One year earlier

I am the lead prosecutor in the office of the Metropolitan Boston District Attorney. I'm known as the attack dog, the top gun, the guy who has blinders on when it comes to the right and wrong of justice. I am that way because my father, "Big Dan" O'Connor, was a captain in the Boston Police Department. There was never any gray in our house; there was only his way or the highway. And there was no sparing of the rod to spoil the poor blind child.

Actually, my da never called me blind. He used words like *sightless, disabled, impaired, handicapped.* I'm not sure why that was. Maybe he just couldn't face the fact that I was blind, or maybe he somehow connected my blindness to his own failure as a man. It wasn't that he was a bad father; on the contrary, he was a good provider. He just never really saw me as I was—and certainly not as I am now.

He's proud of me, no question about it; but we're not close in the way I am with my children, Tommy and Shannon. You often hear that "the sins of the father are visited on the child"—well, I don't think Big Dan O'Connor committed any mortal sins, but I do know that his distance toward me has shaped me into a father who is fully engaged in raising my son and daughter.

Certainly my wife, Bridgette, has a lot to do with the intimacy I have with my family. Actually, Bridgette has everything to do with everything. She is my heart, my eyes on the world, the helpmate and soul mate, friend, mother, lover, sounding board—but I'll talk more about her later.

So here I am, at the top of my game, preparing to deliver the most important summation of my legal career. Life has prepared me well for this important day. First, there was the Perkins School for the Blind in Watertown, where I learned Braille and the skills necessary to function capably as a blind adult. Then there was high school at Boston Latin, the toughest academic public school in the city. Then, somehow my da found the money for me to go to Boston College and Boston College Law School. Not bad for a kid born in a three-story tenement on Second Street in South Boston.

I've spent ten years in the prosecutor's office, putting a fair number of scumbags in the slammer. Along the way, there have been plenty of offers for me to cross to the other side and become a highly paid defense counsel, but I just can't do it. It's not that I feel like a chivalrous public servant, some kind of a knight on a white horse saving the less fortunate from all the bad guys. It's just that—well, I suppose it's just somewhere in my DNA. So thanks, Da.

* * *

I don't think I slept last night. If I did it, was only for a couple of hours. We live in Scituate, a seacoast town nestled twenty-eight miles south of Boston that is often called the Irish Riviera because most of Boston's Irish politicians, along with a few police captains lucky enough to save their money, have summer houses there. Only a few months after Da retired, my mother developed cancer and died quickly. I guess my father didn't want to live in a house full of memories, so he moved to Florida. He sold the house to Bridgette and me, and that's why we can afford Scituate.

And what about my mother? She was a beautiful soul. Where my da believed I should be out in the world with sighted children, Maeve was sure that what I really needed was to get an education and to develop skills that would make me not only independent, but valuable to society. She'd say, "Dan, we have to keep him in the school for the blind. That's where he'll get the support to develop the talents that will make him special." Boy, did they go round and round on this subject. Finally, they compromised and, as I told you, I attended high school at Boys Latin, getting a classical education that has served me well today.

I said that my da's world was always black and white. Well, my mother's was riveted in Catholicism: sacraments and sin followed by confession and forgiveness, saints, feast days, and the cross. She attended Mass every day, never ate meat on Fridays—even when they said we could, continually prayed to the Blessed Mother, and probably believed that sex was something you did only to produce children.

There are three in our family. Two older sisters and me. I love my sisters, but I can't say we're close. I suppose that's because our family never really achieved intimacy, largely due to the fact that my father was so domineering and my mother so religious. We were always afraid to be funny or clever.

5

The rule in our house was, "Don't speak unless you're spoken to." Frankly, that sounds more Puritan than Irish, since the Irish by nature are loquacious communicators. I learned that was true when I went to Boston College and broke out of my enforced shell. I've actually become very outgoing. My job requires me to be a good talker, and thanks to Bridgette and the children I'm totally involved in our community, from helping to coach Tommy's soccer and baseball teams—that's right, a blind guy as a coach—to riding horses with my daughter, Shannon, as she takes riding lessons that cost us too much money.

I've really done my homework and feel completely prepared for my summation. It's great to live in a time when technology has become available to the blind. We have talking everything: computers, GPS, ovens, clocks, thermometers, even baseballs that beep, and our own versions of iPods, iPhones, and Kindles.

But none of those gadgets is as important to my daily life as the astounding animal that lies at my feet. He's an eighty-five-pound golden retriever named Bailey, and though I shouldn't admit it, I love him probably as much as I love my family. He's five now, right at the height of his guide dog talent, and he is everybody's favorite in the DA's office and around the courthouse building. Bailey's personality is an amazing blend of tender and loving, particularly toward my children, with a work ethic that makes him tough as nails when doing his job. Nothing ever draws him away from his fundamental purpose to keep his master safe and to move me efficiently anywhere I want to go.

No city in the world is as complicated to get around as Boston. The streets are laid out like a cow pasture, because that's what it was at the beginning of the seventeenth century. Unlike New York, Washington, and other major cities, there is no pattern to Boston's streets; with my portable GPS and remarkable guide dog, however, I am completely independent. Actually, when I think about it, that's not quite true. Bailey and I are interdependent. That's an important lesson I've learned from my experience with him.

Let me explain it this way: born three months premature, I had a condition called retinopathy of prematurity. There was too much oxygen pumped into the incubator, causing my retinas to be destroyed. I can't imagine what it was like for my parents when they took me to an ophthalmologist for that first examination. This guy had absolutely no bedside manner. After completing a perfunctory exam he simply informed my parents, "Mr. and Mrs. O'Connor, your child is blind, and there may be other developmental complications that will require you to take care of him for the rest of his life."

I don't know what his words did to my parents, but in my quest I became as independent as possible, and I think I have done pretty well. Thank God I was athletic, and sports became my ticket out of darkness. I wrestled in high school and won a state championship. I enjoy skiing and biking with Bridgette and pump a lot of iron at our local health club, so I look good making closing arguments in a well-tailored blue suit. I am computer literate and even do my own taxes.

But my marriage and my life with Bailey have made me understand that I am an interdependent person. Actually, I think that's how it is for all of us. We live in an interdependent world, but sometimes we're just too stupid to figure it out.

* * *

So I'm thinking about a lot of these things as Randy drives me to Boston. My friend Randy is a luxury that my top gun status has allowed. He is a teamster for the city, and he is assigned to me as a driver. This morning he picked me up at four-thirty so I could get to the courthouse a few hours before anyone else.

I'll be summing up my case this morning, and to do it effectively I need to understand my space. By that, I mean I need to plan how I will be addressing the jury. I don't want to come off as blind. I want to be able to move comfortably in the space between the jury box and my counsel table, so I came here early to work on it. I've been in this courtroom before, and frankly I sort of take advantage of a jury. I mean, as I address them, I know I hold their complete attention because they're wondering if a blind guy is going to trip and fall down right in the middle of his summations.

Let's see, it's seven steps from my counsel table to the jury box. I can run my hand unobtrusively along the edge of the box and stop, directly facing individual jurors as I hear them breathing, making them feel that we've established real eye contact. There's a delicate balance in all this. I don't want to draw the jury's attention away from my summation because they're surprised at my mobility, but I want them to feel that I'm competent and that I'm absolutely committed to the belief that the person I am trying to put away deserves it.

So I spend an hour alone in the courtroom practicing. Jane, my paralegal, has also arrived early. She's there not only to help me with the paperwork at the table but to make sure that everything is clear and exactly the way we rehearsed when I stand before the jury and give them my best.

The jury has seen Bailey throughout the trial, but he'll stay with Jane when I deliver my closing argument. I have a feeling we're winning. Jane and my two junior counsels have been watching the jurors' faces, and they informed me that the body language of the jury seems to be in my favor.

I hope so, because this case has become personal. It goes to my core values of faith and trust, values that I've learned through my life experience with Bridgette, my children, and my guide dog, Bailey.

chapter 2

The story goes that Bill Russell, the great center for the championship Boston Celtic teams, always had to throw up before a big game. They call it competitive nerves, and I know it's true. This morning, the butterflies in my stomach were the size of bats as I sat in the courtroom, waiting for the judge to take the bench and call me forward for my summation.

I've learned that there are two kinds of nerves: instructive and destructive. Destructive nerves occur when you doubt yourself or when you doubt the result of the moments to come. Instructive nerves are the good kind. These are when you're saying to yourself, *Bring it on. Let's go. Let's play the game.* And that's exactly how I felt on this morning.

I mentioned that this case is an important one. That's true for a number of reasons. The defendant was Father Edward Gallagher, a priest with a rap sheet as long as your arm for pedophile behavior. Actually, that's not quite true. There was no rap sheet because there was no actual proof until now, though a number of victims had come forward during the Catholic Church's major scandal in Boston, naming Father Gallagher as the pedophile pig who had taken advantage of them. Up until now, all of them had been adults, so the statute of limitations had run out on any criminal prosecution.

Though Father Gallagher was in his late sixties, the monster had struck again, and this time the victim was my client, Alvero Ramirez, a thirteen-year-old Portuguese kid from St. Theresa's parish in West Roxbury, where Gallagher was the monsignor.

The problem with the prior sexual abuse cases against Father Gallagher is that they were circumstantial. There were no witnesses, and medical exams had not been carried out in a timely manner. However, here we had the testimony of a boy who was still young enough to influence the jury, and Ramirez's chilling account of the abuse had been remarkably powerful to these twelve good men and women. His testimony had been supported by the evaluation of a psychologist and a psychiatrist, and his mother had confirmed the ongoing relationship the boy had experienced with the priest.

The defense had worked hard to show Father Gallagher as a true servant of God and his church, pointing out all of his good works during forty years as a priest. Frankly, they had done well.

I had lain awake nights as I prepared my cross-examination. Over and over again, I had pictured myself tearing down the veil of the priesthood, of feigned goodness, which Gallagher wore so easily. But the defense had been smart and not placed Gallagher on the stand, so it would come down to my summation before the jury.

Somehow I would have to walk the line between connecting this case to the problems of the Catholic Church without condemning the Church as an institution. This case was about one man, one priest who needed to be defrocked and locked away so no other child would ever have to suffer the painful consequences of sexual abuse.

The clerk called us to order, and Judge Parker took the bench. He had conducted a very effective trial, allowing enough points to be made while controlling extraneous outbursts that might have influenced the jury one way or the other. When you're a prosecutor, all you can expect is a judge who is fair—because a jury is being asked to weigh the evidence, and a person cannot be found guilty without a preponderance of that evidence, beyond any shadow of a doubt. The way in which a judge conducts a trial largely determines whether the case can be presented effectively, and Parker had done a good job controlling the proceeding.

Seven steps.

"Are you ready to proceed, Mr. O'Connor?"

"Yes, Your Honor," I said, rising.

Five, six, seven—stop and smile. Bridgette had always reminded me that it was important to create visual warmth with the jury, and she liked to say that my smile—even though I had never seen it—could light up a room.

"Good morning, ladies and gentlemen. Thank you for your time and your service in a matter that I'm sure at different points made you uncomfortable, maybe even a little squeamish. We all understand that any discussion that deals with the abuse of a child is horrible for anyone to consider."

I put my hand on the edge of the jury box, leaning closer to the jurors and softening my tone. "I know that during the jury selection process five of you declared yourselves to be Catholics, and it's important for me to note that I also come from an Irish Catholic family. I'm telling you this because I don't want to suggest that the Church is on trial here, though it is necessary for me to talk about certain aspects that involve what I believe a longstanding policy of cover-up and denial."

Taking a step back, I continued, "Let's review what we know

about Father Gallagher. You've heard six witnesses discuss their alleged abuse by this man—they called him a 'monster'—and you've been informed that we have depositions from seventeen other alleged victims of abuse so heinous that we chose not to play you additional tapes that would have only made the same point over and over again.

"This priest—this pedophile—used the power of his office in the sexual abuse of Alvero Ramirez. He did this first by ingratiating himself with the family. He learned that Maria Ramirez was a single mother, which gave him incredible power because he could use the term we all learned as children—'Father.' The power of *Father*. Imagine how that sounded to a family struggling in abject poverty, to children who needed love, support, nurture, and comfort.

"This priest understood all of that, so Father Gallagher began a campaign, first by taking what must have felt like a parental interest in Alvero during the time the child was an altar boy. Then there was the period of gift giving and trips to Red Sox games and the science museum and the *Constitution*.

"Alvero told you of the days when he went to Father Gallagher's room in the rectory and how the hugs turned to touches and the touches turned to kisses and the kisses—you know the rest—turned to events so painful, so demeaning, and so repulsive that I cannot express them effectively in words. But you saw the child's tears, you felt his pain, you experienced the trauma that will live with him for the rest of his life. We can only hope that love and God can ease the burden of shame he will forever carry.

"The psychologists have told you how Father Gallagher convinced Alvero that what he was doing was right and not sinful and how their relationship had to remain their special secret. You've heard from other victims who explained that it often took years before they were able to come forward and express their pain. None of us can imagine how that feels. And then we examined Father Gallagher's record and found that the Church had suspended him three times from parish life and then brought him back.

"I spoke to you about the Order of the Paraclete, the church's internal organization that over the last fifty years has examined hundreds of priest pedophiles and recommended that none of these men should ever return to a ministry that involves interaction with children. There is total recidivism in pedophilia. Once a pedophile, always a pedophile, and this—"

Again, I turned directly back to the priest, willing him to look at my face.

"And this priest pedophile, this 'Father' who abuses God's children and his vows, needs to be removed—not only from any engagement with the innocent but from society."

Now back to the jury.

"You were told at the beginning of the trial that you must find the defendant guilty beyond a shadow of a doubt. Here we have a case largely built around circumstantial evidence that you must weigh honestly. As an example, we presented medical testimony that indicated that Alvero Ramirez was violated by penetration, and wasn't the defense's argument interesting? They suggested that the child probably suffered from some sort of bowel syndrome. I don't think any of us who listened to the little boy here on the stand could ever think that his problems stemmed from any such problem. Circumstantial? Yes. But compelling? Absolutely. So as you consider, remember the testimony of Alvero Ramirez.

"I believe, ladies and gentlemen of the jury, that the choice is clear. There is a preponderance of evidence—though it may be principally circumstantial—that can offer you only one verdict. Guilty as charged."

I turned to the priest and said it again.

"Guilty as charged."

I heard a sigh from somewhere in the jury box and knew that I had done well.

I didn't really listen to the defense, as counsel tried to deflect the impact of my summation in the minds of the jurors. I did not believe there was any possibility that twelve men and women could find Father Gallagher innocent of these heinous crimes.

Following closing arguments, the judge carefully went over the instructions to the jury with the admonishment that they were not to discuss the case or any personal feelings with anyone outside the jury room.

By now it was four o'clock, and Judge Parker chose to dismiss us for the day. The press was waiting outside the courtroom. I told the reporters that Father Gallagher should be put away for a long, long time and that I felt the trial had gone well. Joseph Martelli, the district attorney, was effusive in his praise of my conduct in the case, and around the office I heard "that-a-boy" and "good job" as I packed up my briefcase, called Randy, and prepared to go home to the safety and sanctity of family life.

This was one of those days when I really wanted to go home to Bridgette, Tommy, and Shannon, to wash away the filth of the trial with tender embraces from my family.

As I walked outside, carefully guided by Bailey, I smelled a softness in the early evening air. Though I hadn't been outdoors since early morning, I could sense that spring was about to burst on New England. I looked forward to taking the drive home to my beloved Scituate and enjoying Mother Nature's sensory surprises.

It's easy to get out of Boston, but traffic is still a mess as you work your way down the Southeast Expressway. I was quiet as we drove, and Randy was smart enough to leave me alone with my thoughts. I was reasonably sure that the jury would convict.

Having been raised in a strict Catholic household and attended Boston College with a Jesuit education, I grew up respecting priests and honoring the mantle of Father. But over the years, I had lapsed in my faith. While Bridgette and I were doing a good job raising our children as Catholics and I did attend Sunday Mass, the role of God in my life was hazy at best. I can't say I actively lived a spiritual existence.

As we came to the Norwell exit and turned right on Route 123, I sighed, realizing that I really did need to revisit the question of my faith, but not tonight. What I wanted was to open the windows and take in the spring evening and then get home to the family I loved. Just then, Bailey put his head up on the backseat and nuzzled my hand as if to say, *Don't forget me, master.*

I leaned down and kissed the big dog right on the nose.

"You're a good dog, Bailey. I'm not forgetting you. Hey, Randy," I said, leaning forward. "When we get to the Driftway turn, open the windows back here, will ya?"

"Are you sure, Brian? It's a little chilly."

"That's okay, pal," I said. "I really want to take in some clean air. It got a little dirty in the courtroom today."

"I was there for part of your summation," Randy said. "You were awesome, Counselor."

"Well, let's hope the jury feels that way too. We need to put this guy away so that he'll never, ever hurt another child."

"You got that right," Randy agreed. "Here's Driftway."

Randy rolled the windows down as we turned left and

headed along the two-lane road that would take us into Scituate Harbor. I loved this place for so many reasons. My da had bought the house when I was eight, and so many important moments in my life had happened there. My father had only one hobby—fishing—and it was something we did two or three mornings a week during the summer. He would wake me up at five o'clock, and by six we would be out in the water in his twenty-one-foot sports fisherman searching for mackerel, pollack, and blues when we trolled; bass if we drifted up close to the rocks along Second and Third Cliff; and flounder, cod, and haddock if we used drop lines and fished the bottom. I learned later that the first fish I ever caught, a flounder we named Big Joe, my da had put back on my hook over and over again, making me think that I had bagged at least ten more. That was one time I was glad he had fooled a blind kid, though it was probably pretty tough on the flounder.

I made my first friends in Scituate: twin brothers, David and Johnny Gibson, who moved in next door. We connected across the backyard fence, and the Gibson boys opened up worlds of possibility to a blind child who desperately wanted to be thought of as equal.

Moving along Driftway, I could smell the fresh-cut grass of spring, along with early roses, apple blossom, lilac, and the scent of charcoal from somebody's outdoor barbecue. I could almost taste the air. The ocean's moisture blending with the opening ground was magnificent. I smiled, thinking it was like taking in a good Bordeaux that sits on the tongue and then radiates down your throat.

Being blind isn't bad, I thought, because I could appreciate all of my senses. My sighted friends lived in a world driven completely by vision. Their other senses generally were only in accompaniment to sight, but for me the orchestra was even. Everyone played the sensory song as part of a beautiful ensemble. I had never met a person who was ugly unless he wanted to be, unless that was how he chose to express himself. I didn't operate in a system of labels, and prejudice had never been part of my life. Somehow I had come to the conclusion that I could turn every disadvantage into an advantage and that disability could be an ability if I chose only to try.

As Randy turned left on Jericho Road, the smell of the ocean wafted through the windows. It is, in my opinion, the cleanest smell on earth. Single-cell life clinging to sedimentary rock, along with kelp and weed—there's nothing like it.

And then I heard it: the sound of the bell buoy ringing five miles out on the bay telling me I was almost home. That bell buoy had always been my touchstone. Weather fair or weather foul, you could always tell by the bell buoy's ring. I remember lying in bed on early summer mornings, before my da would come get me to go fishing, and listening to the bell. If the waves were rough, I knew I could roll over and go right back to sleep. Scituate, my paradise on earth. Oh, sure, South Boston had its Irish charm, and Perkins, the school for the blind I had attended, had given me a great education. But it was in Scituate that I was nurtured and nourished, learning to believe in myself and my future.

Randy turned right on Turner Road, and Bailey sat up, knowing we were almost home.

"Hey, Randy," I said, "pull over here, will ya? I think Bailey and I are going to stretch our legs and walk the rest of the way."

"You sure, Counselor? It's pretty dark out there." Randy quickly realized what he had just said, and we both laughed.

"Oh, I think we can handle it, Randy."

Getting out of the car and taking Bailey's harness in my left hand, I said good night to my friend and told the big animal, "Forward."

It's amazing how guide dogs work better at night than they do during the day. Somehow they see every rut and every pothole, and by reading the harness I moved smoothly to the rhythm the big golden retriever established. He would even stop at curbs with my toes just over the edge and give me a little hesitation when we were supposed to step up on the other side. When we turned right on Barker Road, his pace quickened, and he covered the last seventy-five yards to our house almost in a jog.

Bridgette and the children would be waiting. I had called them and told them I was on my way home. They might be eating dinner or doing their homework, but I knew everything would stop when I put my key in the lock, opened the front door, and felt the hugs of a family I knew loved me.

chapter 3

To avoid having my arm broken, I dropped Bailey's leash as I opened the front door, knowing that this was the moment when a hardworking, disciplined guide dog turned into a joyous golden retriever with only one thing in mind—to love as many family members as he could at one time. As I stepped over the threshold and called hello to the family, Bailey was bounding up the stairs in the hope that Tommy would have a ball and the game could begin. Before he could get to the top, eight-year-old Shannon had intercepted him and was being covered in doggie kisses.

I was also being kissed, except the kisses were coming from Bridgette Cleary O'Connor, even more effusive than usual because she understood the importance of what had gone on in the courtroom today.

"You really think you won?" she said, still hugging me. "You think the jury will find in your favor?"

"I do," I said, "but right now I want to forget about all that and concentrate on my wife." Then, raising my voice, I added, "And two beautiful children who'd better get down here and give their dad a hug."

Shannon got to me first. Nothing in the world is like the hug from your eight-year-old daughter when she wraps herself completely around your body as you pick her up and squeeze her. A hug like that, and all is right with the world. My son came downstairs a little more conservatively.

"Hi, Dad," Tommy said. He had just turned eleven, and he tried to keep his voice sounding low to avoid the cracks. "Congratulations."

"The verdict isn't in yet," I said. "We have to wait and see what the jury says. That's our system, and it's the right one."

"Okay, Dad," Tommy said, "but I'll bet you kicked butt."

I allowed a slight chuckle. "You know, Tommy, my boy? I think I did."

I could hear by Bailey's breathing that he now had two tennis balls stuffed in his mouth, probably believing that two was better than one and that maybe both children would play with him.

"Children," I told them, "I'm going in the kitchen with your mother while she gets dinner ready. It smells like meatloaf."

"Meatloaf it is," Bridgette said. "Your favorite, with garlic mashed potatoes and some green beans with almonds."

"Perfect for a hardworking lawyer," I told her, hugging her again. "Thanks for waiting on me to have dinner. Would there be a wee draft of Irish whiskey to go along with that wonderful meatloaf?"

"Come to the kitchen, my boy," she said. "Your whiskey awaits. Okay, you two, back upstairs and finish up your homework, so we can have a good family dinner in about twenty minutes. Oh, and take the furball with you. He's had a hard day too."

Eight feet ran up the stairs, and two in-love adults went to the kitchen.

While Bridgette busied herself with dinner preparations, I sat at the bar and took a grateful sip of the Irish whiskey served by my Irish-American lass in a Waterford Crystal glass.

"Hey," I said, "this isn't just straight old Jameson's, is it?"

"Not tonight, bucko," she said. "First Cabin, Midleton. You've earned it."

"Yes, I have," I agreed. "You know, when the kids were hugging me a minute ago, I couldn't help but think that there but for the grace of God go any of us. I mean, my client is just a kid who was in the wrong place at the wrong time and met the wrong person. Why is that, Bridgette? I mean, why does fate pick one child to go through what that little boy did, while others never face that sort of pain? Is there a plan for all of this stuff we call life?"

"You really want to get into that now?" she asked.

"Well, not really," I said, taking another sip of whiskey. "But just in general, what do you think?"

"I think," she said slowly, "all of this comes down to the role God plays in our lives."

"Hmmm," I said, not wanting to get into a religious conversation.

"Brian, these past few years, I don't think you've thought much about faith."

"What do you mean?" I asked, a little indignant. "Our children are being raised Catholic. We go to Mass on Sundays."

"Yes, but I don't think your faith truly matters to you," Bridgette said.

"I believe in God," I argued gently. "I believe in a higher power, a Creator."

"True, but you don't do anything about it," Bridgette said. "You kind of leave everything up in the air. Your faith is sort of a maybe/maybe proposition with you."

I didn't answer her right away.

Finally I sighed. "Well, I'll tell you this, my spectacular wife, what I do believe in is us—you and me and our two beautiful children up there and a big golden retriever that always reminds us life has to be fun."

Right on cue, I heard Bailey running upstairs as one of the kids threw a ball.

"Look, Brian," Bridgette went on, "nothing is more important to me than our love and everything we share. But life is a lot easier when you have a strong faith in God and when you believe in the power of prayer."

"That's true," I said. "I prayed that you'd come into my life."

"Oh, no, you didn't," Bridgette said, giving me a playful swat with a dish towel. "You're just making that up so we can fool around later on."

I smiled. "Well, whatever works."

"You've always been like that," she went on. "Back when we first met at that Boston College dance, by the end of the evening you were already telling me that I was the kind of girl your mother said you'd marry."

"I did tell you that, didn't I?"

"I'll never forget it."

"But how about what you said?"

"Now that is under dispute," she said, laughing.

"Oh, no, it isn't," I said, coming around the bar and putting my arm around her. "When I told you you're the kind of girl my mother always said I'd marry, you looked right up at me while we were dancing and said, 'Count on it.'"

"I did not," she said, pushing me away playfully. "I would never have told you anything like that."

"Well, didn't you know right from the beginning?" I asked. "Didn't you think I was the only guy for you?"

She put down the dish towel, and I could feel her looking right at me.

"Actually, Brian, you had me at hello. I don't really understand it, but I know it's what happened. I just knew you were the one."

"Destiny," I said. "Fate. Karma. Girl, we were meant for each other."

We were quiet again, both of us understanding the importance of the truth we were sharing.

When I met Bridgette, she was studying nursing at Boston College. We married the summer after we completed our undergraduate work, and Bridgette worked at Mount Auburn Hospital in Cambridge. Along with nursing she was my reader, exercise partner, and lover, and somehow found time to keep our little apartment tidy and still make great meals. I actually gained ten pounds while I was in law school, which was unusual for a starving student. I once asked Bridgette if it ever bothered her that I was blind—I mean, did it bother her that I couldn't see when she dressed up especially for me?

"No," she said without hesitation. "I know you look at me inside out, and that's why I love you."

"Well, the outside's not bad," I told her, and it wasn't.

Bridgette was about five-foot-eight with thick, red hair, dark Irish skin, and big blue eyes. Though I had never seen her in a visual way, I like to think that I understand my wife inside-out, rather than outside-in; although, to borrow a phrase from Ray Charles, Braille ain't bad. I loved her voice because there was always a smile in it; yet when she was serious, her tone could take on the power of conviction. She still worked as a nurse one night a week at South Shore Hospital in Braintree, "just to keep her hand in," she said, but her joy in life came from raising our children and taking care of me—a job she did seamlessly without ever making me feel that I was a burden. There was an intimacy about our marriage that I suppose is unlike many others. It was great fun to watch a movie with Bridgette and have her tell me what was happening on the screen. I loved it when she would read to me or when we'd have conversations over morning coffee that always felt intimate, even if we were talking about something mundane.

On weekends we rode a tandem bike and skied the mountains of Vermont and New Hampshire in the winter. Bridgette had lived in Vermont during high school and was on her local ski team, so she was a strong skier and a fantastic guide. We had decided we would begin to teach Tommy how to guide me that next winter, and I was sure that was going to be a great experience.

What could be perceived as the disadvantage of blindness had become the advantage of intimacy with my family. I participated and got involved in family activities, and there was a true give-and-take of love expressed between people in a family that cared.

It was time for dinner, and eight feet came pounding down the stairs.

As I enjoyed the savory meatloaf, Shannon said, "Daddy, if the kids at school ask me about you, what should I say?"

"Has that been happening?" I asked.

"Sometimes," Shannon said. "When they see you and Bailey walk me to school, they ask about it."

"And what do you tell them, Shannon?"

"Well, if they're nice, I tell them what Mommy says."

"What's that?" Bridgette asked, not remembering.

"You always say, 'Daddy's blind, but God taught him other stuff.'"

"I do?" Bridgette smiled. "That's pretty good."

"And what if they're not nice, Shannon? What do you tell them then?" I asked.

"I tell them to shut up."

"Yeah," Tommy put in, "and you can tell them that your big brother will come over and—"

"Tommy!" Bridgette interrupted.

I couldn't help laughing behind my napkin, and Tommy picked up on it.

"Well, I would. I'd go to those kids and kick butt."

Now I was laughing without my napkin.

"Look, this is serious," Bridgette said. "We can't have Tommy beating people up, and we can't have Shannon defending her father."

"I have an idea," I said. "Shannon, why don't I call your teacher and arrange to come to your school to have a show-and-tell with Bailey?"

Shannon clapped her hands. "That would be great, Dad!"

"Okay," I said. "We'll have a Daddy's day at school." As an afterthought I asked, "Are there other questions some of the kids ask you about me?"

"Well," Shannon said, scratching her chin, "sometimes they want to know if you can see colors. And somebody asked me yesterday what your dreams were like. And some kids want to know about the harness Bailey wears."

"And can you answer most of those questions, Shannon?"

"Sure I can, Dad. I tell them all about the senses too."

When Shannon and Tommy were little, I played a game with them called What's Mommy Doing? When Bridgette would be in the kitchen making dinner, I'd put both children on my lap and have them close their eyes and use their other senses to understand what their mom might be making for dinner. I taught them how to distinguish the smells of various flowers and to listen to music with their eyes closed so they could get more out of its beauty. They love the textures of the ocean almost as much as I do, and they have developed a sixth sense about people that comes from judging their actions, not just on visual cues but taking the extra time to look inside.

As Bridgette passed out the dessert plates, I heard Bailey sniffing, as if he was looking for food scraps on the floor or trying to coax one of the children into giving him something from the table.

"Cut it out, Bailey," Tommy said. "Leave me alone."

"What's he doing to you?" I asked my son.

"Dad, he keeps sniffing me."

"Sniffing you?" I asked, surprised.

"Yeah. He keeps sticking his nose under my arm and sniffing me like he thinks I've got food hidden in there or something."

"Ew," Shannon said. "That's gross! You must really stink."

"I do not," Tommy said.

"Well, actually, you do have a distinct smell," Bridgette said, clinking down his dessert plate, "and it's a wonderful smell. Everyone has their own scent. That's what makes you special." She reached over and ruffled his hair.

I heard the sniffing sound again.

"Bailey, cut it out," Tommy said, a little more agitated.

"Okay, Bailey," I said. "That's enough. Go lie down."

The sniffing came again.

I said, "Go lie down, Bailey," with a little more firmness in my tone.

The dog reluctantly turned and went to the corner of the room, dropping onto the hardwood floors with one of those sighs that says, *Okay, okay, you're the master; I'm just the dog.*

From the time our children were little, Bridgette and I had taken turns putting them to bed so that they shared private time with each parent. Even though Tommy was eleven, he still liked it when I came upstairs with him as he tucked in. As always, Bailey accompanied us, just to get that last hug from the boy.

"Are you pumped up about tomorrow?" I asked.

Tommy was going to pitch his opening day Little League game against the Marshfield Cubs, and I was one of his coaches for the Scituate Indians.

"I'm a little nervous," Tommy admitted. "My stomach feels kind of funny."

"That's okay," I told him. "I was pretty nervous this morning when I was in court. It's okay to be a little afraid. That's what gets our adrenaline going, and we try harder."

"But what if I lose?" Tommy asked. "What if I let the team down? This is a big game. If we beat Marshfield . . . "

"I know," I said. "Everybody thinks Marshfield's the best this year, so if we beat them we might make it all the way to regionals. I know it's a big game, Tommy, but you've pitched before, and you've lost before, and nobody was angry with you. All you can do is your best, and that's plenty good enough for me and for everybody else who loves you—even Bailey."

I heard the big dog sniffing again, and this time he did something he'd never done before. Bailey jumped up on the bed with Tommy.

"Hey, Bailey, what are you doing?" Tommy said, giggling,

loving every bit of it. "Are you gonna stay with me for a while?"

"I bet he is," I said, wondering about the dog's unusual behavior. "You must smell really special today, Tommy. Let me see."

I bent over and hugged my son, making believe I was Bailey and sniffing him all over. He started to laugh, and I added a couple of tickles. That prompted Bailey to lick and slobber all over his face.

I got things back in order and gave my son another hug and a pat on the head.

"Get a good night's sleep, partner," I said. "Tomorrow's a big day. Just kick Bailey off the bed if you can't get enough space. He's a pretty big dog."

"He's okay, Dad," Tommy said happily. "See you in the morning."

"Sleep tight, pal," I told him. "I love you."

"I love you too, Dad," the sleepy voice responded.

I turned the light off but left the door slightly open, so the dog would come out when he was ready.

Downstairs, Bridgette suggested that we watch a little late-night TV and cuddle.

"Now that's an offer a man can't refuse," I said. "Who's on tonight?"

"I don't know," she said. "By the end of the monologue, you'll probably be hitting on me, and it won't matter anyway."

"You've got that right, babe," I said. And that's exactly how it was.

Later, as we held each other in the dark, still feeling the warmth of lovemaking made more pleasurable by deep intimacy developed over years, I said, "You know, Bailey is still up there sleeping in

Tommy's bed. He's never done anything like that before. I wonder what's going on."

"Oh, you're worried about nothing," Bridgette laughed in the dark.

"Well, that's probably true," I said. "But still, I've never seen him do anything like this. An animal's instinct is a powerful thing. Every day I see Bailey do stuff I can't understand. The way he understands what I want or remembers where we've been before and goes right back to the spot is amazing. And then there's the time clock in his head for what I'm going to be doing at any point during the day. He even knows whether the people he meets are dog people or not. Bridgette, there's a lot going on in Bailey's brain that we don't understand, and right now something has him sleeping with Tommy and doing a whole lot of sniffing."

"Whatever it is, I'm sure it's fine," Bridgette assured me, pulling me close to her.

I took a deep breath and drew in my wife's special smell. It was so comforting to know she was there, that I was holding her, that we were together. Her smell, her essence as a woman, was like an enveloping blanket that made me feel I belonged, that I was cocooned and everything was as it should be. Except for Bailey.

chapter 4

Opening day of the baseball season has always been special for me. As a young boy living in the isolation of my blindness, I spent a lot of time in my backyard, listening to kids playing baseball at the Little League field down the street from our house. I longed to be part of their game, to be part of the larger world outside the fence that surrounded my yard. But I was forced to live in my own imagination, supported by the power of radio and the Boston Red Sox.

I would bring a portable radio outside and put it on the back steps of my yard. My father had given me a baseball bat, and I would find rocks on the ground and throw them up in the air, trying to hit them with the bat and announcing myself as if I was a member of the Boston Red Sox playing in Fenway Park. I'll say this for my da, he seemed to understand my passion for the game, and five or six times a year we would go and take in a Sox game together. These were special moments for me, like Christmas or a birthday. My da would buy tickets out in Sun Bums Alley—the bleachers in center field. The seats were cheap, and so were the hot dogs, but the experience of being there with Big Dan O'Connor was worth it.

It was an amazing experience—hearing the sound of the ball popping into the catcher's mitt and the shots that were hit off real wooden bats. Now that was something. Just by listening to the pitcher, I could figure out whether he was throwing a curve or a fast ball by the sound it made when it hit the mitt. What a grand experience.

Twenty-five years later, I was deeply grateful that my son, Tommy, loved the game, and I was living his experience right along with him as his coach. I suppose the idea of a blind guy being a baseball coach might seem odd. I admit that it's impossible for me to catch a baseball and even more difficult for me to hit one. But as they say, necessity is the mother of invention; so when Tommy decided that he wanted to play baseball, I was determined to figure out how I could become part of the game.

All over America, when children begin Little League, they start by hitting the ball off a tee. It's called T-ball. So that's where we began. What I needed to make the game work for us was an outfielder who could retrieve Tommy's hits and get that ball back to me. Who could it be? At that time Shannon was too young for the job, and Bridgette—well, Bridgette had a lot of other things to do just being a mother. Also, wasn't playing baseball how little boys became men and how grown men became more manly?

So who was around to help? A big, young golden retriever with a ball fetish. Bailey was so excited to be part of our game, sometimes he grabbed the ball right out of my hands before I could get it teed up for Tommy to hit. I'd put the ball on the tee and review Tommy's batting stance, making sure he was lined up straight to the target, weight on the balls of his feet, his knees flexed, the bat over his right shoulder and head steady: all the things I'd been reading about from the books I'd read from the library on baseball and batting tips. Then I'd stand back, holding Bailey by the collar, and let Tommy have a whack at it.

I don't like the new baseball bats that kids play with today. They're aluminum instead of maple, and the tinging sound just doesn't seem appropriate. When you hear it, the sound doesn't hearken back to the great hitters driving one over the fence in Fenway Park. But that's modern technology and I suppose "keeping it green."

Tommy would swing, and I'd hear the *ting*, and Bailey would launch off after the spinning baseball. I was always worried that little Tommy might foul one off through the kitchen window, but thank goodness he didn't.

In baseball, there's a thing called a balk. That's when the pitcher starts into his motion and stops. When this happens, the batter gets an automatic trip to first base. In our game, balks occurred because sometimes Bailey wouldn't bring back the ball, opting instead to run to the corner of the yard and try to chew the baseball into a pulp.

To practice Tommy's fielding, we reversed the process. This time I would hold Bailey and throw Tommy ground balls or pop-ups, with the dog retrieving when my little boy threw the ball back to our imaginary home plate. All in all, our backyard ball games were pretty terrific, and Tommy's skills developed quickly.

I wish I could say my maturity as a coach evolved as quickly as my son's talent. I'm ashamed to admit that on occasion I got carried away. So over breakfast on this opening day, Bridgette reminded me about what happened in the championship game the year before.

It was the fourth inning in a 2–2 barn burner, and Tommy was pitching. He had only given up five hits, but his control was a little off, or maybe it was the umpire's calls. It's the same thing big-league ball players complain about: the strike zone. Some umps have bigger strike zones than others, and in Little League you seem to always get the guy who forgets that he's working with kids and calls the game entirely too tight.

To say the least, I'm competitive. So I was willing to offer the umpire my opinions on the game, especially on whether Tommy's pitches were balls or strikes, even though I'm blind.

So there I was, standing in the dugout with Gary Wilson, another dad who shared the coaching duties with me. We decided that the time had come to get on the umpire's back about the way he was calling the game.

"Okay, Brian, here's what I think. If I yell at the guy, he'll probably get upset and make it even tougher on us. But you're . . . " He paused.

"I'm blind, Gary?" I laughed. "You think I have an advantage? So if I yell at the ump, I can probably get away with it, right?"

"That's how I see it, partner."

"Okay. You just tell me what to yell."

And so we began. The problem was, by the time Gary informed me that the pitch was high and outside, Tommy, who was always in a hurry, was into his motion and throwing the next one, so I was always one pitch behind the action. It didn't matter, though, because the truth was I was a loud and obnoxious parent, probably embarrassing Bridgette and Shannon sitting up in the stands, but this was a man's game, wasn't it? Didn't I tell that to my wife later on when she pointed out, rightly so, that these players were only little boys and that I was acting like an idiot?

Tommy threw a pitch that Gary said was a strike at the knees, but the umpire called low.

"What's the matter with you?" I screamed from the top step of the dugout. "You're as blind as a bat!"

Now, coming from me that was quite a thing to yell at an umpire, so I continued. "Can't you get it right? Come on, ump, that was a strike. Open your eyes and call 'em right!"

I had finally gone too far, and the umpire, Ray Martin, a really good guy from the neighborhood, had enough.

"Uh-oh, here he comes," Gary said. "We're in trouble now."

In my excitement I had moved outside the dugout and was right along the first baseline when Ray approached.

"Look," he told me. "I have to take this garbage from everybody in the stands, but I certainly don't have to hear it from you."

"Are you talking to me?" I said, getting right in his face. I went on. "Even a blind guy knows you're calling a bad game. Come on, ump, get it right. You're as blind as I am."

"Let me get something straight," Ray said. "How could a highly successful trial lawyer, someone who is supposed to have great instincts reading people, be such a jerk when it comes to a baseball game played by ten-year-olds?"

"You're blind," I said again loudly, emphasizing it by pointing to my eyes and showing him up. "Blind, do you hear me?"

Now the crowd actually laughed, and Ray had no choice. He made the universal sign with his hand across his throat and pointed.

"You're out of here!" he said. "Maybe I have to take all this crap from the fans, but I certainly don't have to take it from a blind guy."

He turned and stormed back to home plate. And what did I do? Well, I sheepishly called to Bridgette up in the stands to come down and take me away. I can only imagine how Tommy felt as he watched his mother remove his father from the field. We did go on to win 4–2, and I treated the team to pizza following the victory. I also sent Ray a basket of wine and cheese, inviting him and his wife over to our house the next weekend for a peace-offering dinner.

When we got home that night, I went up to Tommy's bedroom and tried to heal the damage in a conversation with my star right-hander.

"Listen, Tommy," I said. "I was completely out of line this afternoon. The umpire is the authority on a baseball field, and no one has the right to disrespect him the way I did."

"I know, Dad," Tommy said. "But the guys thought it was really cool the way you argued. When you got in his face, we thought there might even be a fight."

"Son," I said firmly, "if that's the impression your teammates have about what happened out there today, I'll straighten them out when we get together for practice next week. Sadly, adults are sometimes more childish than kids, and I was way, way out of line."

Tommy seemed to understand.

"I guess nobody's perfect, huh, Dad?"

"You got that right, pal, and I'm a long way from being even close. What I know for sure is that I love you and that I'm trying to do the best job I can to be your father, but sometimes my enthusiasm gets way over the top. I'll just keep working at it, okay?"

"Okay, Dad," Tommy said. "I love you."

"I love you too, son," I said, giving my boy a hug and closing his bedroom door behind me.

And so one year later, here we were on opening day, with Scituate playing Marshfield. Soon I would be back in the dugout coaching, and my son, Tommy, would be getting ready to pitch.

chapter 5

A ll of us were excited as the Scituate Indians took batting practice and warmed up before the game. Our kids had grown up playing against the Marshfield Clubs, so we knew a lot about their personnel. They had some outstanding players and were very well coached, so we figured that if we could beat them it would get us off to a great start, setting up what would be a terrific season.

One of my jobs as a coach was to create a winning attitude with our players. Somehow the parents believed that because I was a lawyer, I had the communication skills to give winning pep talks; so it was up to me to give the team a motivational speech before we took the field.

I honestly can't remember much about what I said that day. I probably talked about teamwork and believing that your teammates would always have your back when the game was close. I know I talked about remembering the fundamentals and keeping your head in the game, but somehow all of that was lost, overwhelmed by the event that would change the lives of everyone in the O'Connor family.

Soon the game was under way, and Tommy was spinning a gem. As we entered the fourth inning, we were leading 5–0.

Tommy already had six strikeouts and had only walked one batter, so I was beginning to get excited about the possibility of lighting up a victory cigar.

"Okay, Tommy," I yelled from the dugout, "just throw strikes, pal. Just throw strikes!"

The chatter from the team behind him was great.

"No, batter, batter, batter! No, batter, batter!" our shortstop yelled.

"Swing, batter! Swing, batter!" our third baseman chimed in.

"Big whiff! Big whiff!" our first baseman added.

"Come on, Tommy! Right to the glove! Hum it right in here. Right to the glove!" the catcher encouraged.

There are moments that play over and over again in your mind, like an old vinyl record with a scratch that just keeps grinding away as the needle digs deeper and deeper into the surface. Sometimes the memory is in a dream or on a night when you can't sleep, tortured by the remembrance of events. Sometimes it comes up in the middle of the day for no reason, and you can almost hear it and once again feel the pain because that pain was so excruciating, so devastating to the person you love most in the world.

I have relived this moment in slow motion many times as my mind has tried to process the reason for it, the why of it. My life has been consumed, mind, soul, heart, and body, with denial that anything so horrific could happen to a little boy—an innocent— my son.

The sound was not the *ting* of an aluminum bat or the crack of an old piece of hickory on a horsehide ball, but a primal scream of pain so penetrating that I froze where I was. I couldn't immediately grasp the import of what had just happened on a pitch thrown by our eleven-year-old son—but Bridgette got it. She told me later that she leaped from the bleachers where she had been watching the game and sprinted headlong onto the field, arriving at the place where Tommy was writhing in agony.

"Oh, my God," my coaching partner stammered. "It's Tommy."

"Tommy?"

I grabbed my friend's arm and we rushed from the dugout as players and managers from both teams converged at the pitcher's mound. Tommy was still screaming in pain, and Bridgette had her arms around him, elevating his broken arm to take the pressure off the bone.

Somebody dialed 911, and since we were fairly close to the Scituate fire station, the paramedics arrived within minutes.

"Where will you take him?" I asked the team leader.

"South Shore Hospital in Braintree. That's the closest emergency room," he told me. "You and your wife can ride in the ambulance with us. It will help keep your son calm. There's a lot of trauma in this kind of break, and I'm sure he's pretty scared."

What an understatement, I thought. One minute Tommy was out there pitching the game of his life, and the next minute they were strapping him onto a stretcher—just another example of how fragile we all are as human beings.

Bridgette asked a neighbor to watch Shannon, and five minutes later we were loaded. During the ambulance ride, Bridgette and I worked hard at trying to ease Tommy's fears. When we arrived at the hospital, the paramedic team moved quickly, and Bridgette and I had to hustle to keep up.

Emergency doctors are traditionally overworked, underappreciated, and often harassed by loved ones who are desperate for answers. The ER attending physician introduced himself as Dr. Don Anderson, and right away I understood that this guy was a no-nonsense trauma care professional. There was no real hello or handshake offered. He got right to the point.

"This looks like a bad one, a break to the humerus," he informed us. "Did I hear someone say that the injury was induced throwing a baseball?"

"That's right," Bridgette said. "Tommy was pitching."

"Unusual," the doctor muttered. "Okay, let's get him over to X-ray and see what we can find out."

I put my arm around my wife. We encouraged Tommy to stay strong. The doctors were going to fix him up, and we'd be close by at all times.

"Listen, let's step outside," I suggested to Bridgette. "We could use some air, and we probably ought to get out of the way so that these guys can do their job."

We went outside and sat on a bench at the far end of the building with a gurgling fountain that had been placed there to create a peaceful environment among the hubbub.

"How could this have happened?" Bridgette asked, taking my hand. "How could a trauma this severe have happened to our son just by throwing a baseball? It doesn't make medical sense."

I could feel that her hand was wet from wiping her eyes, and I knew she had been crying.

"I don't know," I told her. "There are a lot of big leaguers who blow out their arms, but I don't know about anyone, big league or otherwise, who broke their humerus. Usually it's something in the wrist from throwing a curve ball or a slider. Frankly, Bridgette"—I squeezed her hand—"I don't understand this at all."

We were quiet, both of us absorbing the thought but not knowing where to go with it. We stayed that way for a while—just holding hands and waiting.

I could sense that Bridgette kept her eyes on the door, watching for the doctor to reappear inside. A few minutes later, he did, and we crossed the patio to join him. He stepped through the door and took a big gulp of air.

"Mr. and Mrs. O'Connor," he said, "I've called in an orthopedic surgeon to evaluate the break, but I have to tell you, I don't like the look of it. The orthopedist will have to check it out, but I believe he'll be ordering a CT scan, an MRI, and maybe even a bone scan."

"What do you mean, a bone scan? It's just a broken arm," I stammered.

The doctor tried to allay my concerns. "Dr. Weinstein will be able to provide a lot more information. He's a terrific surgeon, and I'm sure he can answer your questions."

I couldn't help wondering if that was doctorspeak for "It's serious." Was Tommy dealing with something more critical than a broken bone? I could feel the chill run up my spine and Bridgett's hands go clammy as we waited for the surgeon's arrival.

The sound of quick steps and the smell of expensive Polo aftershave preceded Dr. Weinstein's brusque entrance.

"Mr. and Mrs. O'Connor, I'm Dr. Benjamin Weinstein," he said.

I reached out to shake hands and was given only his fingertips in response, as if my touching his miracle hands was an affront to his talent.

As he began to speak, I sensed that he never made direct eye contact, and his monotone was even less than what could be described as a no-nonsense professional approach.

"Mr. and Mrs. O'Connor," he went on, "your son has a transverse fracture of the upper humerus with severe trauma to the area. There is major discoloration and extensive swelling, suggesting a far more dynamic episode than throwing a baseball would generally present. At this time, I have chosen to splint the arm and keep it immobilized while we continue to evaluate the extent of the injury. I've given your son morphine for pain, as proximal arm fractures can create a great deal of discomfort. I'm ordering a number of tests—CT scan, MRI, and a bone scan—to be done over the next few hours."

Bridgette interrupted. "Doctor, I'm a nurse. Can you tell us why you're not setting the bone?"

"Because there's too much immediate trauma to the area, Mrs. O'Connor. As I told you, the episode should not have prompted such extensive damage, so we're going to keep your son overnight to avoid what we call compartment syndrome."

"Compartment syndrome?" I asked. "What does that mean?"

I could feel the doctor's patronizing smile.

"Mr. O'Connor, compartment syndrome," he explained, sounding like a college lecturer, "occurs when there is extensive swelling and bleeding into the tissue, causing too much pressure on all of the nerves and vessels in the area. Remember, this is a major trauma injury, so it needs to be treated appropriately. In fact, I believe your son should be moved to Children's Hospital in the morning, and in preparation I've contacted a pediatric orthopedist to consult and take over his case."

"Children's Hospital?" I said, sounding surprised. "I know it's a great place, but it sounds like you have major concerns about Tommy. The ER doctor told us that he didn't like what he saw. Are you confirming that?"

For a moment the arrogant tone was gone. "I'm saying that I want a pediatric orthopedist, someone who does this all the time, to define the appropriate course of treatment."

Bridgette pressed him. "In my experience, when a doctor uses a phrase like 'course of treatment,' it suggests a lot more complication than a simple broken bone."

The doctor sighed. "Listen," he said, "I'm going to look at the tests and then consult with Dr. James Erickson at Children's. He'll take it from here. You can pick up Tommy in the morning to check him in, and I've set up an appointment with Dr. Erickson in the afternoon."

The doctor abruptly stood, turned, and headed for the door. Opening it, he spoke over his shoulder. "Good luck, Mr. and Mrs. O'Connor." And then he was gone.

We sat for a long moment, stunned. Eventually we regained our composure and spent the next few hours helping Tommy go through what would become an all-too-familiar experience of CT scans, the banging of the MRI machine, and the discomfort of bone scans, all handled bravely by our little boy.

When the ordeal was finally over, Bridgette called our neighbor and made arrangements for Shannon to spend the night. When she handed the phone to Shannon to let us tell her good night, we simply told her that Tommy just had a broken arm and he would be just fine.

Then we got Tommy settled as best we could in his hospital bed with some ice cream and the promise that we would stay with him all night.

Over the next few hours, as Tommy tossed and turned, Bridgette and I didn't talk and only ate a cold tuna fish sandwich from the cafeteria to keep up our strength. It was as if we had pulled inside ourselves, tensed by the possibilities that loomed out there, even though we had no idea what they might be.

* * *

When I woke up at 3 a.m., Bridgette was tapping on her iPhone, deep in concentration.

"What are you doing?" I asked, gently.

"Looking for possibilities," she said.

I put my arms around her shoulders.

"Don't do that," I told her. "The second you begin that process, you create nothing but more anxiety."

She turned to face me. "I can't help it, Brian. Call it my instinct as a mother or my nursing background or something, but I know this is bad, really bad. I just feel it."

I touched her cheek and noticed that my hand was shaking. "I'm feeling the same thing," I told her. "But whatever is going on with Tommy, we'll face it together, like we always have. Let's try to get some sleep."

Bridgette sighed. "I don't think I can sleep. I'm just too frightened."

"I know, dear. Me neither. Maybe we can just hold each other."

And that's what we did, sitting there in the cold hospital room wide awake, listening to the ticking of the clock and Tommy's even breathing, knowing that the time would come soon enough. Morning would give us the answers we dreaded to hear.

chapter 6

Before Tommy was awake, Randy picked me up, and I went home to pack toiletries and clothes Bridgette would need for what we believed might be an extended stay at Children's Hospital. I also wanted to stop in to say hi to Shannon and assure her that everything was okay, even if I didn't believe it. Bridgette had arranged for her parents to take Shannon to their home for a few days in order to let us completely focus on Tommy and Children's Hospital.

I wanted to return to the hospital as quickly as possible, but traffic along Route 3 headed north from Scituate crawled at a snail's pace. I found myself drumming my fingers on the dashboard of the car as Randy drove. I wanted to get to Tommy, I wanted to get to Children's Hospital, and most of all I wanted answers.

Bridgette met Randy and me at the elevator, and I could tell she had taken on the quiet demeanor that meant she was pulling inside and gathering the strength to cope with whatever the doctors might say. I wondered why we were both feeling so negative about Tommy's diagnosis. We had no concrete reason to believe that something was profoundly wrong with our son—at least, not yet—it was just a broken arm. Yet somehow in the hours we had held each other the night before, we seemed to be acknowledging our tacit belief that our family was in crisis.

After thanking Randy and sending him home, Bridgette and I went to the nurses' station to fill out paperwork. By the time we completed Tommy's forms and finally arrived at his room, our Tommy had had enough of South Shore Hospital. He even seemed offended when they made him take the obligatory wheelchair ride out into the brilliance of a grand New England day.

Ridding himself of the chair, Tommy got into the backseat of our car, and I heard him struggle with the seatbelt, having to fasten it left-handed.

"Want some help, pal?" I asked him.

"I'll get it," he said irritably.

And I listened as he grumbled to himself, finally snapping the belt into place.

As we continued up the Southeast Expressway, I was taken completely off guard when Tommy asked, "Hey, Dad, why do I have a splint on my arm instead of a cast? And why are we going to another hospital?"

Thankfully, Bridgette, the nurse, answered his question.

"Tommy, there's a lot of swelling around the injury," she told him, "and the orthopedic surgeon doesn't want to set the bone until all of that has gone away. We're going to Children's Hospital because they need to run some more tests, and the doctor you're going to see is a pediatric orthopedic surgeon." And then she added, "A specialist in children's injuries."

Tommy sounded irritated. "I know what 'pediatric' means, Mom. So I need more tests because these guys aren't sure, and the problem with my arm may be more serious? Is that what you're saying?"

"Sorry—yes," Bridgette said. "I forgot I had the smartest boy in the world for a son."

"You got that right," I put in. Trying to lighten the conversation, I added, "Along with being the best right-handed pitcher our Little League has ever seen."

"Do you think I'll pitch again this year, Dad?" Tommy asked, his voice a little shaky.

"Well," I said, biting my lip, hoping he didn't see it, "I don't know about this year, son. You know, these kinds of fractures take a long time to mend. But very often when a bone is broken, it becomes even stronger after it's healed."

Tommy then asked the question that had kept Bridgette and me up all night. "How could this have happened, Dad? I mean, I've never heard of anyone breaking their forearm throwing a ball."

"Well, Tommy," I said, "it's one of those freak accidents that nobody can understand. I guess it's something that just happened. What's important is that we take care of it and get you right back to throwing fastballs again."

Bridgette pulled into the underground parking garage for Children's Hospital. Then we began the endless process of paperwork that would dominate so many hours of our lives—medical releases, insurance forms, health history, income statements, and other various and sundry legal releases. Just filing out the paperwork seemed to take forever. And the interminable waiting. The three of us experienced firsthand that our health care system was overburdened, and it seemed that the gears of process had ground to a virtual halt.

Finally, after waiting four hours, we were told that Tommy would be getting a bed in the pediatric ward on the fourth floor.

"In, oh, let's see," the admissions person said, "in about three more hours, give or take."

So we sat in the waiting room, and time moved at a pace slower than morning traffic. It was late in the afternoon when we finally checked Tommy into his room and then got another surprise. The orthopedist we would be seeing, Dr. James Erickson, had ordered another MRI.

"Why wasn't the one Tommy had at South Shore Hospital good enough?" I asked the supervising nurse on the ward.

"Well, Dr. Erickson likes the way our techs and radiologists handle the imaging," she said. "We just like to get it right here at Children's."

I didn't doubt the truth of what she was saying, but I wondered as an attorney if this wasn't just another legal protection in case the patient was unhappy with the way he was treated.

Anyway, my speculation didn't mean much, and it was dinnertime before we accompanied Tommy back to his room after the MRI. The one positive of the day was that one of us would be allowed to stay with Tommy through the night, and we had decided that Bridgette would remain. Bailey, my guide dog, had been alone for a good part of the day, and I needed to feed him and give him some TLC. So I called Randy and arranged for a ride home.

I almost made the mistake of hugging Tommy too hard as I said good-bye, but the hug I gave my wife had a feeling of—what was it?—desperation, I think. We had gone through an entire day in this place knowing nothing. It would be another sleepless night and another morning before we would see the pediatric orthopedic surgeon in the early part of the afternoon of the third day since Tommy's accident.

For as frustrated as I was and as emotional as I knew my wife was feeling, we hoped that our young son was somewhat immune from the concern that weighed so heavily on his parents.

Randy and I didn't talk on the ride home, but it was wonderful to see Bailey when I put the key in our front door, opened it, and was nearly knocked over by the jumping, turning, licking, and loving golden retriever who lived only for his master.

That night I broke a family rule and allowed Bailey to sleep on Bridgette's side of the bed. I just felt like I needed to hug someone I loved, and that night Bailey was all I had.

After a fitful sleep, I got up at 5 a.m. and decided that Bailey and I both needed some exercise. One of the blessings of having a great guide dog is the ability to go where you want, when you want, and at what speed you want.

From the time I got Bailey three years ago, we became morning joggers—not anything overextended, because dogs should never run too long at a time. A veterinarian had told me that it's because dogs can only sweat through their tongues and feet, so on long runs they tend to overheat. Actually, a dog can run much farther than a person if allowed to run at its own speed. What I mean is that when dogs run free, they can fly ahead for a couple of hundred yards, sit and wait for you to catch up, and then run again. But Bailey was a guide dog, so our runs forced him to operate at my pedestrian pace. Still, he loved our morning runs, and though our course was still shrouded in darkness, the big animal could guide me perfectly along the quiet streets of Scituate.

On this day, we ran out to Minot Lighthouse and stopped at the point to take a breath and absorb the sensory panorama of the morning. At this early hour the ocean was calm as glass, more peaceful than I could ever remember it. Neither the bell buoy nor the foghorn was active, and the seagulls' cries suggested that they thought it was going to be a good morning to dive for breakfast.

I sat on a bench that Bailey had found, with the dog at my feet, and tried to decide if I was prepared for whatever the day would bring.

I had coped with the disappointment and difficulty of disability all my life, yet the blessings I'd received through my relationship with Bridgette, my children, and my career far outweighed any negatives I had experienced along the way. True, my mother was dead and my father was distant, but everybody has stuff to deal with, don't they? And my problems didn't seem to be overly burdensome, except now. This crisis involved something out of my control—something affecting the son I loved—and I was scared. No . . . that wasn't really right. I was frightened out of my mind.

Why? I asked myself over and over as I sat on the bench. *Why am I so frightened?* Because the orthopedic surgeon at South Shore Hospital had played it safe. I could tell from his manner that he believed there was much more to Tommy's broken arm than he was willing to admit. My instinct as a lawyer told me that. How often had I grilled witnesses I knew were lying or holding back the truth? Even a blind man could tell from the doctor's body language and manner that he was not completely forthcoming. He didn't make eye contact with me. I knew that because I could hear his voice coming from a different angle. His chin was down, and he repeatedly moved his shoulders in what I believed must have been a shrugging motion. Also, he rubbed his hands together two or three times as he framed the conversation. In other words, "I'm passing the buck on this one, Mr. and Mrs. O'Connor. I'm going to let someone else drop the hammer on you. It's going to be another doctor's problem."

And so I sat on the bench, afraid, patting the big dog's head to try to gain some assurance.

On our way home I ran faster than usual, wanting to test the limits of Bailey's guiding skills, wanting to assure myself that I could do anything, handle anything, survive anything. *Aren't I Brian O'Connor?* I kept telling myself. *Aren't I a winner? And more than that, aren't I married to the wonderful Bridgette? And don't we have a great little boy who has all the right stuff to make it through anything?*

"Okay," I said to Bailey as I got dressed and waited for Randy to arrive. "Let's go see Tommy and take care of this."

At the name Tommy, the dog's tail thumped the floor.

"That's right, boy," I said. "We're going to see Tommy, the little kid you love."

Dr. Erickson met us just after lunch and after completing his rounds on the pediatric ward. We met in a conference room, and I was immediately struck by the contrast in style between the surgeon we had dealt with at South Shore Hospital and this big man with a gentle presence, who gave me the impression that he loved children and hated the injuries and diseases they suffered from.

"Mr. and Mrs. O'Connor," he began, "what did Dr. Weinstein tell you about your son's break?"

Bridgette answered. "He said that it was a difficult fracture, Doctor—a transverse fracture—and that because of the swelling around the area, he was not prepared to set the bone. He told us that's why Tommy's arm was only splinted and why he referred us to you."

"Okay," Dr. Erickson said, "that's correct. It is a transverse fracture. Let me pull it up here on the screen so we can all take a look at it. Oh, I'm sorry," he said, catching himself. "Mr. O'Connor, I just wasn't thinking."

"No problem, Doctor," I told him, and it wasn't a problem. What it was—what I really hated—was that I couldn't see the screen, that I couldn't participate and directly understand what Tommy's injury represented. The doctor tried to make amends.

"Look," he said, "I'll do the best job I can at explaining this to both of you. A transverse fracture transects the bone. That is, the break is vertical rather than horizontal. The doctor at South Shore was telling you the truth when he said that a break of this kind causes massive amounts of swelling and discoloration. You can see it reflected here on the pictures, Mrs. O'Connor."

"Yes, I see it, Doctor," Bridgette said.

"So why does this happen?" I asked. "I mean, why does this kind of transverse break cause such swelling?"

"Well, Mr. O'Connor, that's a good question. You see, a fracture of this kind disrupts the blood supply to the bone so the body works at trying to compensate, and so we find this kind of major swelling."

What he said next set off an alarm bell in both of us.

Tapping the screen, he said, "This is a pathological fracture."

"Pathological!" Bridgette said immediately. "You mean there may be a disease involved?"

"Well, yes, I am, Mrs. O'Connor, but let's not get ahead of ourselves. I'm going to explain something to you now that I know may frighten you. But I want to be very clear that what I'm about to say may or may not have any real consequence. By pathology, I mean that there may be tumor found in the bone."

"A tumor?" I repeated, my voice shaking.

"It's possible," the doctor said. "Tumors like this happen proximally—that is, in the top third of the bone. Mrs. O'Connor, as you can see from the picture, Tommy's break is right there in the top third of the humerus. Also, you can see that this is a spiral fracture, rather than a displaced fracture. This suggests that the injury as reported was underproportional to the level of fracture we are seeing."

"You mean it shouldn't have happened?" I said.

He paused. "Yes, that's what I mean, Mr. O'Connor." He went on. "Mrs. O'Connor, I want to point out something to you that I think you'll be able to see clearly isn't right in the cortex of the bone. If you look very closely, you'll notice a periosteal elevation."

"What's that?" I asked.

"Well," he continued, "with a regular bone you can see a nice straight line along the edge, very uniform in context and texture. When we see periosteal elevation, there is a little elevation that looks like a triangular plateau on the bone, kind of a shard of osteo tissue—a bump on the bone, as it were. Can you see it, Mrs. O'Connor?"

"Yes," Bridgette said. "I can see it."

Next, Bridgette surprised both of us by taking my hand and saying, "So what you're telling us, Doctor, is that you're concerned that this could be a malignancy."

The doctor was taken aback, and I wasn't willing to grasp what my wife was saying.

After a pause he said, "Yes, Mrs. O'Connor, that's exactly my concern."

"Wait a minute!" I said, my voice rising. "What are we saying here? Somebody tell me what all this means."

My wife answered the question for the doctor.

"We're discussing cancer, Brian." The word hung in the air between us. "Our Tommy may have cancer."

Dr. Erickson tried to allay our fears. "It is true that Tommy might have cancer, but there are a number of kinds of tumors that can be found in a bone. The ones that are benign are called aneurysmal bone cysts, and they are very easy to handle. We just scrape out the tumor material and then get to the business of setting the bone, and that's all there is to it."

"Doctor," Bridgette said, "we need to know the whole story, all of the other possibilities."

"I'm getting to that, Mrs. O'Connor," the doctor said, "but let me tell you first that until we take a biopsy and get it to the lab, we really won't know much of anything. I'm going to order other tests because often when we take a frozen section, the initial reading is not complete. There are procedures that have to be done on the bone in the lab for us to really know the answers, and frankly it can take a few days to complete the pathology. While that's going on, I'd like Tommy to have chest x-rays and some other tests."

"Why is that necessary?" I asked.

"Because we have to be sure," the doctor said, measured. "We have to be sure that if there is a tumor, and if the tumor is cancerous, that there is no further spread of the disease."

I felt like fainting. I was dizzy, and the doctor's words didn't seem real, like they were coming from another universe, a place I didn't want to live in, a place where Tommy and Shannon and Bridgette also didn't belong. But we were sitting in this conference room, and a very caring physician was telling us that our son might have cancer and that the cancer might have spread somewhere else in his little body.

I forced myself back to the moment.

"You see," Dr. Erickson said, "when the bone broke, that

trauma may have sent tumor cells throughout Tommy's system. That's why we have to do more tests—we need to know whether the tumor is localized. But please remember what I said before. The chances are more likely that this tumor is benign, nothing more than a bone cyst."

I hung on to his words like a man suspended by his fingertips over the Grand Canyon, and I could feel by Bridgette's grip on my hand that she was doing the same.

Again the doctor was speaking. "I want you to understand that what we'll be talking about is what doctors call a differential diagnosis, or choices in the medicine. We're going to look at a list of possibilities for a given set of symptoms and findings from the tests, so when we get the results back on Tommy and do a complete workup, we will then reorder all of the possibilities. The MRI will give us that information, so we'll probably know immediately whether there is or is not a tumor—but as to the type, I'm sorry to tell you that we won't know about that until the lab work comes back.

"Please, let me now explain the two types of tumor we may be dealing with if our findings indicate a malignancy.

"The first type, osteosarcoma, is very easy to see on an MRI because it creates mass and has a lot of bony calcium-type features. In bones we sometimes find stuff we call osteoid. It's a special kind of material that's unique in its cellular development."

"You mean in cancer cells?" I said.

"Yes," he said. I could tell from the direction of his voice that he was not looking at me directly but going on. "So, as I was saying, osteosarcoma is very easy to see. Ewing's sarcoma is the other type. We call it 'the artful dodger' because it presents a destructive tumor that breaks up bone but really is difficult to identify because there is no obvious mass in the area.

"Right now this is what we know: there was and is an obvious weakness in the area of Tommy's humerus. That's why the trauma was so severe, based on the nature of the injury that occurred. But until we complete the biopsies, we really won't know anything. Frankly, there are many times when I wish I didn't have this conversation with parents until we could get all of the biopsies back. It creates a level of worry that's wrenching for everyone involved."

I heard Bridgette nod, and I slumped deeper into my chair.

Bridgette asked, "Dr. Erickson, can we bring Tommy home after you've done the biopsy? I mean, if we have to wait a few days for all the tests, there doesn't seem to be any reason for him to have to stay in the hospital."

"Well," the doctor said, "unfortunately, Mrs. O'Connor, because we're taking other tests to deal with the question of metastasis—chest X-rays, for example, and more bone scans—it would be better for Tommy to say here in case we decide to begin immediate therapy."

"You mean chemotherapy?" I said, not believing I was asking the question.

"I don't think we should get ahead of ourselves," the doctor said. "It's much too early. We're just trying to remain proactive by doing all of the necessary testing."

"Let me understand again, Doctor," I said. "After the MRI, you're going to do a chest X-ray to look for metastasis?"

"That's right, Mr. O'Connor. We call it a chest CT, but as I said we're also going to do another bone scan. Maybe it would be helpful if I explain the difference in all of these tests.

"A CT scan is a pure look at the anatomy. It's electronic imaging that gives us cross-section slices of the area of interest. With our computers, we can home in on certain features of the tissue that may suggest indications of bone versus suspicious tissue.

When we do an MRI, we gain extremely valuable information about how tumors function. We can learn something about the molecular and biochemical features of how the tissue is actually performing. This can be very helpful in distinguishing tumor molecular activity from the activity surrounding a simple cyst, which you remember means a completely inactive event.

"We also will use a bone scanner to look at every bone in Tommy's body. Here we'll inject radial nuclei into the bloodstream, and then the material will find bone. Once the chemical has bonded, we put a scintigraph over the area. The scintillator is a round disc that's about the size of a hula hoop, only it's thick and hangs suspended over the body. Then, as it passes over the body, it registers whether the material has a sparkling nature that suggests highly active cells. We do this test over an extended time period, meaning in sections. So that's another reason Tommy has to remain in Children's."

I found myself lost in doctorspeak as I struggled to get hold of this complex information. I hoped that Bridgette, the nurse, was getting it all. What I was hearing was that Tommy was very sick, and all of these tests would probably only confirm the fear that gripped my heart.

"I'm sorry that this is so complicated, but there's just no simple way of explaining the technology. I'd like you to know that I'm very proud of the fact that this hospital has a policy allowing the parents to be with the child during every test. Tommy will never have to be alone. You can be right there with him at all times."

I heard the doctor take off his glasses and turn back to where we were sitting.

"Look, I can only imagine how you're feeling. Please, let me express again that I'm here for you in every way. And that goes for all of my colleagues, the nurses on the floor, and anyone else we may be have to call in to make Tommy better. I want you to remember, that is our goal: to make your son better. If the tumor is benign, there's no problem—and if it's malignant but localized, Tommy has an excellent chance for complete recovery."

Over the next few hours Bridgette and I kept trying to lift each other's spirits, working to pull each other out of the mental and emotional abyss that seemed to be welling up around us. We reminded each other that we had a little girl to deal with and that we would soon have to explain to Tommy why he was going to remain in Children's Hospital.

Over coffee, Bridgette seemed to be reverting back to her training as a nurse. She said to me, "Okay, we're in this battle now, and we have to deal with Tommy's issues one moment, one day at a time, one procedure at a time. Do you understand that, Brian? That's what we have to do."

I agreed with her, but my mind just couldn't get past the crushing gravity of what we had learned from Dr. Erickson. Our little boy might have . . . could have . . . there was a possibility of . . . cancer, and every time I acknowledged the word the feeling was like being shot in the stomach at close range by someone whose intention was to commit murder.

chapter 7

As Randy snaked his way through morning traffic, I realized there was a lot I had to catch up on. Over the last few days I hadn't even thought about my professional life, and there was a little girl I loved more than life who needed my attention.

Her words tumbled out through the cell phone I had pressed to my ear.

"How's Tommy? I miss you, Daddy. Where's Mommy?"

"Hi, princess," I said. "Everything's fine. Mommy's at the hospital with Tommy helping him take some tests. I'm on the way there now. Are you doing all right with Gramma and Grampa?"

"Oh, yes, Daddy," Shannon said. "Last night we played Scrabble, watched TV, and ate a whole lot of ice cream."

"That sounds pretty good," I told her. "Maybe you don't ever want to come home."

"Oh, Daddy," she said, and I could tell she was smiling. "I want to come home right away."

"Well, that makes me happy," I told her. "It'll just be a couple of days, and then we'll all be together. We just have to fix Tommy's arm, and then we'll be right back home again. By the way,

Mommy called your school, and we're getting your homework assignments so you can keep up with your class."

"Aw, do I have to?" she said.

"Yes, you do, young lady. It's better to do your homework now than fall behind. It will make life a whole lot easier."

"All right," she said. "I'll do my homework, and you get Tommy home quick, quick, quick. Okay?"

"Okay," I said, hoping that was the truth. Then I added, "I love you, Shannon."

"I love you, too, Daddy," she said.

We hung up, and I sat back for a minute, thinking about how I would explain to Shannon if her brother had . . . And I couldn't use the word.

Memories of Tommy, *my* Tommy, flooded my consciousness. Snapshots—an odd phrase, I thought, for a blind person to use, but that's what these were for me—pictures of moments when love was shared. I remember holding my son as a baby and touching him gently, understanding for the first time how a little human was actually formed.

As the car continued along Route 3, I vividly remembered what it felt like as my fingers touched the smoothness of his baby skin; his head, with that special misshape that reminds us that coming into this world can be difficult; his newborn smell, so baby-like and pure. Then there was the first time he said "Dada" and the way he reached for me as Bridgette filmed his first steps. And the way he held my hand, always understanding the simple truth that I was blind. And how he learned to lead me effortlessly, without difficulty or embarrassment.

Tommy is a verbal child, and I believe it comes from all the nights I spent telling him stories and sharing conversation. I smiled as I remembered our wrestling matches and the bouts of tickling that would often go on until both of us were sore from laughing. And then there was the sharing of the senses on the long walks we took together along the beaches of Scituate, picking up shells and examining them, talking about all the seabirds we could hear, and listening to the crashing waves that Tommy learned to describe in the same way I did.

No father and son could be closer. But now every time we hugged good night, I found myself shivering. I couldn't help wondering about the permanence of those hugs.

I shook my head, working to clear it of any negative thoughts, and placed a phone call to the district attorney, my boss.

I hadn't even thought about the jury's decision regarding the pedophile priest, knowing that my associates would be in the courtroom covering for me.

"Hey, Joe," I said, getting the DA on the line. "I'm sorry I haven't been communicating. It's just that, well, Tommy's circumstance may be more severe than a simple broken arm."

"Don't worry about it," Martelli said, surprising me with his warmth. "The jury came in late yesterday afternoon. The only Mass your priest will be saying from now on will be to the prison population of Walpole State, because that's where he's going for a long, long time. Great job, Brian. Take all the time you need with your son. And what do you mean the broken arm could be worse?"

"Oh, it's just complicated," I said, not wanting to talk about it. "The break—it's just a little more complicated."

"Well, you call us if you need anything," he said. "We'll keep the wheels of justice turning until you come back."

"Thanks, boss," I said. "Thanks a lot."

* * *

When Bailey and I arrived at the hospital, the nurse on Tommy's floor informed me that my boy was scheduled for the biopsy procedure in about an hour.

I called Bridgette on her cell phone and told her I was upstairs at the nurses' station.

"I'll come get you," she said. "I think it's really important that we're both with Tommy when he goes in for the procedure. I'll tell you something, Brian, he's kind of freaking out. He just doesn't understand the idea of a biopsy."

"That's a hard one, Bridgette," I told her. "It's hard to explain to him why this procedure is happening, without telling him that we're worried. We're just going to have to tap-dance for a little while until we get the results."

"All right," she said. "I'll be right up to get you."

"Oh, by the way," I added, "I had a chance to talk to Shannon on the way in this morning. She is doing just fine with your mom and dad. By the time we get her home, she'll be completely spoiled."

For the first time in a couple of days Bridgette laughed, and I loved the sound.

"I'll be right there," she said, hanging up.

As we rode down the elevator to radiology, I put my arm around my wife. "You must be pretty tired."

"It's not lack of sleep," she told me. "It's the not knowing. It's just . . . It's just so hard."

And right then, on an elevator, my wife shattered. She fell into my arms, the tears pouring down her face and soaking into my shirt, her body convulsing with sobs.

"What if it's cancer? What if Tommy has cancer? I should have noticed. I should have seen it! For God's sake, I'm a nurse. Why didn't I know my son was sick?"

I held her even closer. "Listen, Bridgette, this is all happening so fast, and there were no obvious signs, at least to us. Maybe Bailey smelled something wrong with Tommy—you remember we read about those dogs who seem to be able to detect cancer—but the doctors aren't even sure if he has cancer. We just have to wait and see. So let's just keep believing he doesn't."

The elevator came to a stop, and thankfully when the door opened no one was waiting to enter.

Bridgette asked, "Do you mind if we make a stop before we see Tommy? There's a chapel on the first floor. Could we go in there for a minute?"

"Sure, that's fine," I said, not really meaning it.

Though it was nondenominational, the chapel did have a central altar, and we knelt at it, two people coming from very different places regarding faith.

Bridgette was intense, ardent in her prayers. I could tell, listening to the sincerity of her whispers as her lips moved, entreating God, begging Him to make Tommy okay.

My prayer was much simpler because my belief was much less committed. I hoped God was on our side, but I wasn't the kind of person who counted on any form of divine intervention. Maybe my blindness had made me too self-reliant, I wasn't sure, but prayer had never been a critical part of my life. I was sure that it wasn't something you could just turn on because you need it, so my minimalist prayer was in support of my wife's remarkable faith.

"Hi, pal," I said, coming up alongside Tommy's gurney.

Tommy nearly jumped off the table. "I don't want to do this, Dad. Why do they need a piece of my bone?"

"Because they have to figure out how to set it," I told him, lying through my teeth. "This is a bad injury, Tommy. You just threw that baseball too hard, and we have to fix it."

"But why are they looking at a piece of my bone, Dad? How will that help them know how to fix my arm?"

"Tommy," Bridgette said, "you've met Dr. Erickson, the man who is going to do the surgery. Remember?"

"Yes," Tommy said.

"Well, didn't you think he was a nice man? I did. And I'm sure he would never do any procedure he didn't need to. He only wants to make you well and make sure your arm is as good as new."

"That's right," I said, trying to help. "Maybe if we get the bone fixed right away you'll be able to pitch in a couple of months, in time for the playoffs."

That seemed to satisfy Tommy, and we arrived at the operating theater with no more protests coming from our son. We both hugged him gently as they took him into the operating room and we sat, as all parents do, waiting for the procedure to be concluded.

"I talked to Dr. Erickson," Bridgette said, sitting beside me on the worn vinyl couch. "He told me that this would be a simple excising of the piece of bone and that the procedure would take only about twenty minutes. Then they'll look at a frozen section and talk to us if there is any conclusive information on the pathology."

"Let's just hope that it's a simple cyst," I said.

"Just a cyst," she repeated.

We were quiet for the next forty-five minutes, both lost in our own thoughts—or maybe I should say in our numbness. I had coped with blindness and learned to turn my disadvantages into advantages, but at this moment I could find no solace or possibility any-where, except in the thread of hope that we would wake up from this dream and our lives would go back to being normal. Finally Dr. Erickson appeared, still in scrubs.

"Well, folks," he said, "the surgery went just fine. But I have to tell you that after looking at the frozen section, the result is incon-clusive."

"So that means there's either no tumor or it's Ewing's sarcoma. Is that right, Doctor?" I asked, my entire being on hold.

"Yes," he said. "I'm afraid that's the way it is. We have to wait for the lab results. Hopefully, they'll only take a day or so. Let's stay positive, Mr. and Mrs. O'Connor, and we'll see."

And that became our mantra while we waited—*Let's stay positive.*

We also worked very hard to keep Tommy positive. Over the next two days, I don't know if any little boy has ever played more video games or watched more movies than Tommy. Yet nothing we did could make him comfortable remaining in the hospital, not understanding why he was there and worrying about what was to come.

Finally we got the word. Dr. Erickson wanted to see us at two o'clock in the same conference room. All the tests were completed, and the pathology was back.

So there we were—a caring physician and a husband and wife, balancing precariously on the edge of a precipice, hoping not to fall.

As we took our seats, I became aware of another presence in the room, and Bailey confirmed my suspicion as he laid down next to my chair with his head turned to the left and his ears up in anticipation of greeting a stranger.

"Mr. and Mrs. O'Connor," Dr. Erickson began, "I've invited a colleague, Dr. Jennifer Hennessy, to join us."

"Good morning, Mr. and Mrs. O'Connor," she said with a Boston accent even thicker than mine.

"Good morning," Bridgette and I answered together, wooden in our response, waiting for Dr. Erickson to begin.

He got right to the point. "Mr. and Mrs. O'Connor, I wish I had better news for you, but after examining the tumor under the microscope and viewing all of the pathology, the conclusion is that Tommy's tumor is malignant. A Ewing's sarcoma."

For a moment the world stopped turning. I don't think I moved or breathed. I was alive but at the same time dead, frozen—not willing, not able to grasp the gravity of the life-changing pronouncement Dr. Erickson had just levied on our family.

I reached out, desperately trying to connect to Bridgette, but she was already speaking.

"Then it is cancer," she said. "Tommy has cancer."

Dr. Hennessy responded. "Cancer," she repeated. "It's a frightening word, Mrs. O'Connor, but I want you to know that we have a lot of experience dealing with tumors of this kind. I'm a pediatric oncologist, so based on Tommy's test results, Dr. Erickson called me in to help get Tommy well."

I had the sense that these physicians had played this scene together many times before, yet I did not doubt their sincerity.

Dr. Erickson took over. "Dr. Hennessy is considered one of the foremost pediatric oncologists in the country, and I want you to know that Tommy is fortunate to be here at Children's because of its direct affiliation with the Dana-Farber Cancer Institute. Farber is part of the Children's Network, along with other hospitals like St. Jude's that I'm sure you've heard about. We share common information concerning the disease and any breakthrough in treatment in protocols. I believe Tommy is in the best possible place, and I'm one hundred percent sure that you will never find a more committed physician than Dr. Hennessy."

"Thanks for the glowing endorsement," Dr. Hennessy said, "but really, Mr. and Mrs. O'Connor, my job is to gain your trust and along with the rest of our team try to make Tommy well. If you're able to hear this now, I would like to tell you where I think we are."

I nodded, so the doctor continued.

"The minute any doctor uses the C word, the anxiety level of parents rises exponentially. You're probably feeling numb at this moment, so as we have this discussion, please stop me anytime and ask questions. Repeat them if you need to until we are absolutely clear together on where we are and on Tommy's course of treatment. Okay?"

"Okay," Bridgette said, and I nodded again.

"Well, let me first share some good news. I'm pleased to tell you that all of our tests indicate that there has been no metastasis of the tumor. By that, I mean we do not believe that cancer cells have traveled outside the site through Tommy's bloodstream."

"So the tumor is localized," Bridgette said.

"That's right, Mrs. O'Connor. We believe that the disease has not spread beyond Tommy's upper arm."

I leaped on the doctor's words like a starving animal finding food. "Are you telling us that Tommy has a good chance of beating this thing?"

Dr. Hennessy was measured in her response. "As I said, Mr. O'Connor, we have a lot of experience treating tumors of this kind. Frankly, I don't like to talk in percentages because each case is different. What I'm willing to say—what I'm comfortable telling you—is that we have had great success treating tumors like this. There are a number of complex factors that have to be assessed over time, but I believe Tommy has an excellent chance to survive and go on with his life."

I've always been the kind of person who needs specifics, details, closure on an idea. Maybe this arose out of the insecurity of my blindness or out of my training as a lawyer. I wasn't sure, but I wanted more from the physician.

"I understand, Doctor. I know you said that you don't like to speak in percentages, but please give us your best estimate."

"If you're pressing me, there is maybe a seventy to seventy-five percent potential for cure."

I exhaled audibly. Maybe I had been holding my breath for a long time. I wasn't sure.

"Then where do we go from here?" Bridgette asked.

"Well, the basic outline for treatment will involve three potential modalities," the doctor told us. "First, we'll begin with chemotherapy in order to shrink the tumor. Then Dr. Erickson will perform surgery, and there is an excellent possibility that down the line we will employ radiation directly to the site.

"I want to talk to you about the initial chemo stage. This will be utilizing a number of medicines that have had success in combating this kind of tumor. We call it a 'cocktail,' but in a way that's a bad use of language because there's nothing fun about it. I'll get to the side effects in a few minutes.

"The therapy will be carried on over a number of weeks. Around the country hospitals and oncologists make slightly different choices in terms of a cycle, but here's what I want to recommend for Tommy. The initial therapy will be administered over a four- or five-day period, depending on Tommy's tolerance of the drug. Then there'll be nine or ten days off with a renewal of therapy using different medicines for probably three days. Again, there will be a break of eight to ten days, and then we will renew the process again. This will happen a number of times until we are confident that we have shrunk the tumor and that there's no metastasis of the disease in Tommy's system. Let me add that we'll change the drug regimens so that the tumor will not develop resistance. These cells are incredibly smart, and we have to constantly surprise them in order to kill them.

"Now I want to talk to you about the drugs we're recommending. In all of the Children's Hospitals around the country we are constantly trying to upgrade our medicine choices—by that, I mean add to the number of available drugs. Here's how we approach this issue. We recommend that Tommy be placed on the drugs that have been having the best results over recent periods, but along with that we also recommend that Tommy enter a phase-three clinical study in which two experimental drugs are offered. Now, part of the study is blind in that Tommy will be receiving one or the other of the drugs, but the choice will not be predetermined. By doing this we're able to evaluate the success of the new medicines."

Bridgette's tone was sharp. "What you're telling us, Doctor, is that you'll be using experimental medicine on our son. Isn't that what you're saying?"

I could tell that Dr. Hennessy had heard this before.

"You're right, Mrs. O'Connor," she said. "There are no absolutes in this war we're fighting. If there were, we would be able to predict with far more certainly Tommy's outcome. The truth is that through your son's treatment we're trying to learn more about how to cure the disease, not just in Tommy but in other children. Let me be very clear on this point. These are phase-three drugs that have been studied extensively and have shown not just promise but very positive results.

"I love children, Mrs. O'Connor. I'm not some mad scientist trying to get my name or this hospital's name into the medical journals. My concern first, foremost and always, is your little boy. And my job is to compete with this horrid disease and beat it."

The intensity in Dr. Hennessy's voice made Bridgette and me both take the first step to believing Tommy was in the best possible hands. I raised a question for both doctors. "Why can't chemotherapy come after surgery? I mean, if this tumor is localized, why can't we just cut it out?"

Dr. Erickson answered the question. "Mr. O'Connor, as I've already said, we don't believe there has been metastasis, but because Tommy's humerus was broken, there still is the possibility of spread. We begin with chemo, first to reduce the size of the tumor, making the job of the surgeon easier; and second, as Dr. Hennessy noted, we want to be absolutely confident that we have contained any metastasis."

Dr. Hennessy went on. "What we want to do now is bring Tommy into the operating room, and Dr. Erickson will install a central venous catheter in Tommy's chest. This will allow us to pump medicines into his system. We also will be able to easily withdraw blood that we can constantly test. The particular catheter we're going to install is called a double lumen catheter. By that we mean two tubes that allow us to send our chemo drugs through one side and use the other for other things like antibiotics, pain medicines, or even anesthesia if necessary.

"I'd like to clarify what we're trying to do here so that you aren't in any way confused. When we use the word *cancer,* we're talking about cells that replicate at a rapid rate and have no appropriate mechanism to stop the growth. In effect, they are runaway cells, so when we place Tommy on chemotherapy, what we're doing is interrupting particular points in the replication cycle of these runaway cells. In effect, we're attacking the basic DNA of the cell to disrupt its machinery of production. That's why we use different drugs at different times.

"The cells hide deep in the body in a phase we call G-zero or growth-zero state, so when we provide the patient with medicines that attack the active cells and kill them, we prompt the cells in the G-state to go active, and consequently we keep attacking what's left. I know this sounds complicated, but it's important that we're all on the same page regarding the need for such intense therapy.

"Now I need to explain the effects of all of this therapy on Tommy. Let me speak a little more about cells. One of the problems with chemotherapy is that it not only goes after the cancer cells, but it also kills the cells in the body that normally grow and divide every day. We have two sets of cells that are important to understand—cells in your blood and cells in your gut. It's amazing to consider that every week a human being replaces all the cells in the GI tract. Our bodies are terrific factories.

"Your bone marrow makes three basic kinds of cells, and all three types of cells are interfered with when we administer chemotherapy. Tommy will be regularly receiving transfusions, even if nothing is necessarily wrong with his blood. He will also be receiving medicines to prompt the bone marrow to keep making cells.

"Our biggest risk during chemotherapy isn't from taking the drugs, and it isn't even from the tumor. It's from infection because, simply put, you lose all of your infection-fighting cells along with killing the cancer. I suppose this is the trade-off we're forced to live with. You see, we can give transfusions for the red blood cells that carry oxygen and platelets throughout the body, but you can't transfuse the white blood cells, which are necessary to fight infection. That's why it's an exceptional problem in cancer patients. I've often heard people say that cancer is an overabundance of white cells. Actually, in the case of tumor that's not true, but the cells produced still have the same effect, because if we can't get the tumor under control, at some point the cell growth chokes off a vital organ. So you can see it's quite a battle."

"Dr. Hennessy," Bridgette said, "in my nurse rotation I've seen chemo administered, and I know there are major side effects. I think it's important for you to give us a preview of what we might expect with Tommy."

I heard Dr. Hennessy sigh. "This is the worst part of my job, Mrs. O'Connor, as I'm sure it is for you as a nurse. You never want to see children sick, and it's difficult to accept the idea that we have to make them sick in order to make them well. But anyway, I'll tell you about the usual side effects.

"First, we'll premedicate Tommy for nausea. We've found that some kids are prone to vomiting and some are not, but all of them have nausea, even though our medicine is pretty good. Somewhere around the third or fourth day of treatment, he probably will develop mucositis. These are terribly painful ulcers in the mouth that make eating almost impossible. A lot of kids drop weight during this period, and we have to supplement their food intake through an additional nasogastric tube. So we give them meds for pain, and there are side effects from the meds.

"Because of all that, it's likely that Tommy will stay in the hospital during the first two rounds of chemo. We also will have to deal with something called neutropenia. This means a low white cell count. This is when fever spikes on a continuing basis. Frankly, Mr. and Mrs. O'Connor, this is an ongoing problem, and you have to be prepared to deal with it throughout Tommy's course of treatment. We will try to get him home as often as we can, but neutropenic fever is an element we struggle to control.

"Let me put it this way. We are constantly going to be trying to maintain a balance of good white cells, and there are two important types. These are called neutrophils and lymphocytes. The lymphocyte cells make antibodies to fight infection, and neutrophils eat bacteria. While Tommy's having the chemo, his body won't have the capacity to fight bacteria, not just externally but internally.

"Look, I understand that I'm painting a very dark picture. I'm not a physician who sugarcoats what's going on here, but the end goal is to make Tommy well again. And as I said, we've had a great deal of success here at Children's Hospital competing against these tumors, and that's exactly what the team and I intend to do for Tommy: compete with the cancer for his health. Listen, I know you're nervous about Tommy's reactions to chemo and the use of radiation. It's all scary. But really, Mr. and Mrs. O'Connor, we have the best people here at Children's, and all of them are committed to making Tommy well again.

"I suggest that you both take some time to talk together. This is a lot to take in, I know. But it is important that we begin to treat Tommy right away, so I hope you will be prepared to start tomorrow."

"Doctor," I asked, "do you have any thoughts about how we can talk to Tommy about this? I mean, how we can tell him he has . . . " I paused, not willing to say the word, as if the disease would become more real if I named it.

"Well, there are a couple of approaches, Mr. O'Connor. One is for all of us to tell Tommy together. If we take that approach, I'm sort of the lead dog. I mean, I'll be the person who uses the words and delivers the message. Sometimes that's easier for families. In other cases, this is a decision that the parents make for themselves: they share the conversation as a family.

"The truth is there's no perfect answer, and all we can do is the best we can do. So take some time and decide for yourselves. Dr. Erickson and I will wait for your answer."

I stood, along with Bailey, wanting to get out of that space—wanting to get outside and breathe some fresh air, to clear my head—but I knew that would be impossible.

I remembered what Bridgette had said earlier, that we would have to operate one day, one hour, one moment at a time in what was going to be a war to defeat cancer and save the life of our son.

chapter 8

When Bridgette and I fell in love during our days at Boston College, we often walked along the bike path bordering the beautiful Charles River on the Cambridge side. There was something so peaceful in this pristine collegial environment: the magnificent buildings of Harvard; the Half Shell, home of the Boston Pops; Boston University; and the Children's Science Museum bordering the river.

All of it had been part of our falling in love, so at this moment of turmoil and turning point, we drove to the river to walk, even though the rain was coming down in sheets. Thankfully Bridgette had an umbrella, but I don't know that it would have mattered. And for Bailey, a true yellow Lab, water was his favorite thing. The pounding rain and the northeast wind allowed us to be isolated in our grief—alone on the river—feeling empty, vapid, with no idea how to cope.

Tommy had cancer. Like the rain soaking through our shoes, the reality was finding its way into our minds, our guts, our hearts, the marrow of our bones. As we walked in silence, I tried to will myself to think clearly—to come up with a plan. The first order of business: how did we feel about Dr. Hennessy becoming Tommy's principal physician?

"So what do you think of Dr. Hennessy?" I asked Bridgette.

"I think we're lucky, Brian," Bridgette said. "When she was talking about how much she hated the disease, I wish you could have seen her eyes. She means it, and I believe she brings her best to her job."

"Good," I said. "I also felt that she was very organized and knew what she was talking about. I think she explained things very well, and I think, in general, she offered us a positive prognosis."

"I agree," Bridgette said.

"So we're okay with our doctor, right?"

"Yeah, I think so."

"Have you been giving any thought to how we should handle our schedules? I mean, being with Tommy?"

"It seems overwhelming," Bridgette said. "You know, we've still got Shannon to take care of, and you've got a job."

"I know. I've been thinking about that. I have four weeks of vacation time and, I don't know, maybe thirty days of sick leave. That'll get us through the first couple of months, and then . . . well, then I guess we'll just have to see. Do you think your mother would be willing to stay at the house? I mean, just move in for a while to take care of Shannon? I think it's important that Shannon continue to go to her own school. We've got to try and keep her life as normal as possible."

"I agree," Bridgette said, "and I'm sure my mother will be there for us as long as we need her. I think we probably should alternate nights at the hospital so that we both have time with Shannon."

"Yeah, that's what I was thinking," I said. "I could probably make a deal with Randy to continue to drive me there, at least for a while. Maybe that would be okay with my boss, for me to keep using Randy. If not, I'll try to hire him privately or use a different car service. There's also the boat that runs from Cohasset right into downtown, and I'm sure there must be bus service. And I've got Bailey here to help me get around. We'll work it out."

At that moment I banged my fist into the palm of my hand, hating my blindness and the inconvenience it caused.

Like the rain, our conversation seemed to be getting harder. I took a deep breath of the cool, moist air, filling my lungs and trying to clear my head.

"So," I said, my arm around Bridgette, "how do we tell him?"

"I don't know," she said. "I just don't know. Like the doctor told us, there isn't any right way, but I think we need a plan. We need to be definite about the way we explain it to him, and we have to be together on this."

"I agree," I told my wife. "So should we be direct? And if we are, how do we make it seem positive? Wasn't that what the doctor also said? Be upbeat and only tell Tommy what he really needs to know?"

"So does that mean we tell him he has cancer?" Bridgette asked, her voice shaking.

"I think that's a truth he has the right to hear," I said. "Even an eleven-year-old boy needs to understand that he's very sick."

"All right," she said, "but what about all the side effects of his chemo? Does he have to know about those right now?"

I took another deep breath. "I don't think so, Bridgette. That's like telling a child the bogeyman is coming tonight. I mean, let's not put things in Tommy's mind that will make him worry and upset him. The real deal is going to be tough enough, and it seems to me we'll have to try to handle the side effects as they show up."

"Okay, so we're going to tell Tommy he has cancer. Should we explain that the doctors believe the tumor is just in his arm?"

"I think so. I think that's part of the optimism that Dr. Hennessy was talking about—giving Tommy something positive to hold on to so he can survive when the side effects of the chemo get tough."

Bridgette shivered, but I didn't think it was because of the rain. The import of what we were saying seemed to be gripping us in cold, clammy hands.

"Hey," I said, "aren't we right near the Sonesta Hotel?"

"That's right. How did you know?"

"Well, do you remember how they used to put a flagpole out front? In this wind you can hear Old Glory waving, and I know that right in there they have the best clam chowder in Boston. Let's go in and warm up. What do you think?"

We went through the doors of the inviting hotel and settled at a small table in the café, ready to enjoy some of Kenny's famous clam chowder. I thought about having a drink but decided against it, opting instead for a hot cup of coffee. We were quiet while we ate. I suppose we felt there was nothing more to say. We knew what was coming, and we dreaded it. Maybe we were galvanizing our strength in order to be as positive as possible with Tommy.

For the first and only time I don't think I even tasted Kenny's award-winning soup. I just ate it. And then quietly we walked back out in the rain, found our car, and drove back to the hospital.

Tommy was watching *Shrek* when we entered his room. He turned it off immediately and asked, "What did the doctor say? When's he going to fix my arm and let me go home?"

"Take it easy," I said, trying to create an atmosphere. "One question at a time, pal."

"Dad, I just want to get out of here," Tommy said. "Hospitals aren't any fun. I want to go home. I even want to go back to school."

Bridgette forced a laugh. "Now that's something," she said. "I've never heard you say anything like that before."

"Listen, Tommy," I said, feeling my stomach knot up and bile rush into my throat, "your mother and I need to explain something to you, and it's important that you pay attention. Okay?"

I could feel my son turn to look at me, and I was sure his eyes were saying, *What is it, Dad?*

"Well, when we talked to the doctor, he explained that it was unusual for you to break your arm that way when you were throwing a baseball. That's why they did all those tests, to try to figure out what made the bone break the way it did. What they learned was that you have a tumor in your arm."

"A tumor?" Tommy asked, not really getting it. "What do you mean, Dad?"

Bridgette jumped in.

"Tommy," she said—I could hear her sitting down beside him and putting her arm around her little boy—"the tumor that's in your arm is cancer, so we have to keep you in the hospital for a while to get rid of it. Tomorrow the doctors will begin to give you some medication through a tube they're going to put in your chest. The medicine kills the cancer cells, and it makes sure that there aren't tumors anywhere else in your body."

"I have cancer? Am I going to die?" Tommy asked, his voice breaking.

"No, no," I said, reaching out for my son. "You're not going to die. Dr. Hennessy says"—and I lied—"Dr. Hennessy says you're going to be just fine."

I spoke with conviction, wanting to believe it myself. "And

you are, Tommy. You just have to stay here for a while and take these medicines."

"And one of us will be here with you all of the time," Bridgette said. "We're going to get rid of this cancer together, Tommy— Mommy and Daddy and Shannon. We're going to help you get rid of this cancer together."

At the sound of Tommy's name, Bailey got up from the floor and, as if he understood the importance of the moment, licked Tommy's hand.

"See?" I said. "Even Bailey's going to help. Tommy, a lot of people get cancer, take the medicine, and then they're just fine. I know it's awful to be in the hospital and to have your arm in a splint, but your mother and I will be right here with you. And we'll all help you get through this. Okay?"

"Okay," Tommy said, his voice shaking a little.

Bridgette went home later that night to be with Shannon, and I was amazed at the resilience of our son. Tommy dug into the ice cream he had with his dinner and even enjoyed watching the Red Sox play the Tigers on television in an early season night game.

We didn't talk about cancer again until just before Tommy went to sleep.

"Dad," he said, after we turned out the lights and I settled down on my cot. "Dad?" he asked in the dark. "Are you afraid?"

How to answer such a complex question? I wondered, and then I quickly decided. "Yes, Tommy," I said. "I'm afraid, but I think we can handle this cancer because you're a strong little boy, and I believe that if people love each other enough, that's the most powerful medicine there is."

I was surprised when Tommy continued the question. "Okay,

Dad, but does God give a kid cancer? I mean, does He know I have it?"

In that instant, I clearly understood I was not the person to answer this profound question. Faith was a commodity I simply didn't have, so I took the easy road.

"Tommy, I don't believe we're smart enough to know what God thinks. It's sort of a mystery, but I'm sure we have the strength to get through this together. I love you more than anything, so I figure that's good enough. Good night, pal."

"Good night, Dad," my little boy said. "I love you."

I waited until I was sure Tommy was asleep, listening to the rhythm of his slow breathing and feeling the importance of every breath he took. Rising quietly and telling Bailey to stay, I stepped into the corridor and used my cell phone to call Bridgette. She answered on the first ring.

"I was hoping you'd call," she said. "I haven't been able to sleep."

"Join the club," I told her. "But it isn't just because of Tommy. Do you realize we've had very few nights apart during our thirteen years together? I don't do very well like this."

"Neither do I," she said softly. "You sure feel a lot stronger when you're holding the person you love."

"I know. I guess we're going to have to get used to being apart while we take care of Tommy. How did you do with the princess?"

"Oh, Brian," she said, "Shannon was so happy to have me home. It made me feel good to know that our little girl really needs her mother."

"Family," I said. "There's nothing like it."

"And that's what we have to hold on to, Brian," Bridgette said, her voice taking on clear definition. "We have to believe in the strength of our family. And we have to put our faith in God's love and willingness to help Tommy."

"I was just telling Tommy that," I said. "I was telling him that nothing is more powerful than love."

"Not even cancer," she added.

"Not even cancer," I echoed. "So you'll be here in the morning?"

"Yes," she told me. "I have the alarm set for five. I'll eat breakfast with Shannon and have my mother take her to school. That will get me to you by about nine. Tommy's procedure is scheduled for noon, so there's plenty of time."

"Okay," I said. "Try to get some sleep."

Sleep didn't come easy that night, and my dreams were nightmares full of doubts and fears.

We're just humans, I thought in a fitful waking moment, *fragile, delicate human beings inside and out.*

Morning would come, and then the biggest challenge of our lives would begin.

chapter 9

The next morning, Dr. Erickson installed a central venous catheter in Tommy's chest.

"It was routine," he informed us afterward. "A simple surgery. No complications."

No complications? I thought. *My son has a thing in his chest, and he's going to be attached to tubes, poisoned by drugs, and fed intravenously. And all because he has cancer.* Even though I understood clearly what the doctor meant, no "simple" procedure could have more complex possibilities than this routine surgery performed safely in Boston's Children's Hospital.

Coming out of the procedure, Tommy was moved from his room on the pediatric floor through a long tunnel that connects Children's Hospital to the Dana-Farber Cancer Institute. For me, the tunnel felt like an allegory for families when their children are shuttled over to Farber. *Is there light at the end of the tunnel? Is there hope at the end of the tunnel? Is there life at the end of the tunnel?*

I was thinking all of those things as Tommy was checked into his room, and the first of the drugs—the poisons to kill a poison—was pumped into his system. Within three hours, Tommy was overwhelmed with nausea, and we found out quickly that he was one of the vomiters, as projectile vomiting wrenched his system and caused him to cry out loud. As I held a pan for him I tried not to cry myself. Bridgette put cold cloths on his forehead, held his hand, and tried to soothe him.

Bridgette and I wore masks to prevent infection, and I suppose, symbolically, we masked our fear by talking about inane subjects. When Tommy wasn't vomiting or sleeping, I babbled on about the Red Sox and their start to the season. I also talked about the Celtics play-off run and how Tommy's Little League team had been doing in their last three games. Bridgette tried to engage him by reading stories, but all of our efforts quickly ran out of steam as Tommy struggled with the nausea and discomfort of the chemo needed to keep him alive.

I had experienced substantial frustration coping with being blind throughout my life, particularly when not being able to see made it impossible for me to achieve a goal, but that could not compare with the feeling of impotence and ineptitude I experienced as we sat beside Tommy's bed hour after hour watching (and hearing) our child suffer.

Ironically, though the doctors could not predict the direction the cancer would take in the human system, their forecast concerning the reaction to the chemo was right on. Three days into the first round, Tommy developed mucositis, horrible sores in his mouth, and he could barely eat.

Dr. Hennessy and her team were terrific. Whether it was her oncology fellow or her pediatric residents, everybody was caring and completely supportive of us. Yet Bridgette and I felt so alone behind the masks we were forced to wear in order to avoid compromising Tommy's immune system.

On the fourth night after the commencement of therapy,

Tommy was so sick that we broke the hospital rules, and Bridgette and I both stayed in his room—with Bridgette on a cot and me in a chair, along with Bailey taking up a new position on the floor as close to the head of Tommy's bed as possible.

There had been some conversation with Dr. Hennessy about whether the big animal should be allowed to stay in the room, but we all decided that the love he offered Tommy was worthwhile. And I was amazed as I listened to the dog's interactions with my son. They had always been close, but now the usually rambunctious yellow Lab was careful, quiet, and completely attentive. All Tommy had to do was make eye contact with Bailey, Bridgette told me, and the dog was instantly up on his feet, no doubt wondering if there was anything he could do, offering help and affection in whatever way Tommy might desire.

Bailey didn't even seem to want to go out during the days when we were there. In fact, when I did take him downstairs to relieve himself, there was no desire for a game or time to run around. All he wanted was to get back to the child he loved, nearly pulling me into the elevator and down the hall at breakneck speed.

By day five I was sure that every white cell in Tommy's body had been destroyed, both good and bad. Dr. Hennessy examined Tommy and determined that the boy had had enough, and so we began the nine- or ten-day cycle with love and medicine to re-up the white cell count.

Tommy surprised us by bouncing back, and by day eight Dr. Hennessy was saying that we might even get a couple of days at home, being careful to give us that information only when we were outside in the corridor. Tommy didn't hear about it until the end of day nine.

"Hey, pal," I told him, smiling behind my mask, "Dr. Hennessy is going to let you come home for a few days. What do you think of that?"

"Yeah!" Tommy said enthusiastically, the sores in his mouth creating a lisp in his speech.

"The thing is," Bridgette told him, "you're going to have to eat to keep your strength up."

"Okay, okay," Tommy said. "I'll eat anything. Just let me go home."

It was a beautiful day as we pulled into our driveway. Early June in New England. I don't believe anything is quite like it. The ground is opening up, and the smells and textures of the air become a potpourri of creation's greatest perfume.

Tommy got out of the car before it actually came to a stop, and Shannon was right there to greet him. I know I should have been conscious of the potential for infection, but in that moment when brother and sister hugged and Bailey ran in circles around the two of them, I didn't have the heart to interfere. They went upstairs to share video games, and their laughter sounded through the house with a happiness that had been lacking during the last agonizing weeks.

For the first time in a great many days, Bridgette's voice took on a lightness. "You know," she said, "Tommy's homecoming is on a very special weekend."

"What's that?" I said.

"Come on," she chided. "Tomorrow is June eighth. What happened on June eighth?"

"Oh, wow," I said, a little ashamed. "Shannon's birthday."

"Right," she said, "and we have to make it extra special."

Bridgette's mother took the opportunity to return to her own home for a couple of days, and I was reminded that she had another life and that she was sacrificing so much on behalf of the O'Connor family.

"Call me if you need me," she said as she drove away. "I can get back here in an hour."

"Thanks, Mother," I said. "I don't have the words to thank you enough."

"Well," she said, "this just makes the old man appreciate me a little more while I'm gone. You know, you men need us to do that every once in a while."

I laughed, and it felt good. "Well, thank Charlie for me, will you? His best girl is an amazing person, and I'm glad she's my mother-in-law."

"You weren't a bad choice for my Bridgette," she said, beginning to back out of the driveway. "Not a bad choice at all."

I was smiling as I went back into the house.

Bridgette made Tommy's favorite dinner—meatloaf with mashed potatoes and gravy, along with mixed vegetables and a chocolate ice cream pie that he had loved since he was very little. He tried to eat, but not very much went down. His mouth was just too sore, and the chemo had devastated his appetite.

Still, after dinner our family felt almost normal as we talked, watched a movie, and then went through our nightly routine of putting the children to bed. Only this time, Bridgette and I did not divide the exercise. Together we tucked them both in, and as it had been just before cancer imposed itself on our lives, Bailey insisted on sleeping in the room with Tommy, and, as when I let Tommy hug Shannon, I took a chance and allowed it.

In hindsight maybe I was wrong, but there just aren't any absolutes when learning to cope with this disease, because you're trying to create a sense of normalcy in the chaos it imposes.

For the first time since we learned about Tommy's cancer, I was asleep. I mean *really* asleep. Out like a light. Dead to the world. Until the world—our world—came crashing in.

Tommy stood next to my bed with Bailey right behind. His hand was touching my face, and it was warm. No. As I jolted myself awake, his touch was *hot.*

"Tommy," I said, "are you all right?"

His voice was shaking. "No, Dad. I'm burning up."

I put my arms out in the dark and hugged my son and knew immediately that we were facing the dreaded neutropenic fevers that Dr. Hennessy had told us about.

Now Bridgette was awake, and the nurse in her took over. "Call my mother while I get Tommy dressed," she ordered. "We've got to get back to the hospital."

"No," Tommy said, the tears falling from his eyes and soaking my undershirt. "No, not the hospital. I want to stay home. Please! Just get me the medicine from Dr. Hennessy and let me stay here."

"We can't do that, Tommy," Bridgette said gently. "We can't run the risk of infection. You have to be on antibiotics so that you're strong when you have the next round of chemo."

"I hate cancer," the boy said, his anguish ripping my heart out. "I hate it."

Now Shannon came into the room. "Tommy," she said, "are you okay?"

"I hate cancer," Tommy said again, and I realized with searing clarity that we had not yet explained cancer to Shannon.

"Call my mother, Brian," Bridgette said again, "and please take Shannon with you."

I suppose we were all crying at that moment when I picked up Shannon. I could feel her shaking with sobs. I carried her downstairs and held her as I called Bridgette's mother and filled her in. Then, awkwardly, I tried to explain cancer to my little princess.

"Shannon," I said lamely, "cancer is like a bad germ in Tommy's system, and it eats a lot of the good things that Tommy needs to be healthy. The medicine the doctors give your brother kills the germs, but it also makes him weak, so he gets a fever. When his temperature goes way up, we have to keep him in the hospital to give him the right kind of medicines."

"Will he be okay?" Shannon asked through her tears.

"Oh, sure," I told her, remembering Dr. Hennessy's comment about putting a positive spin on the illness, "he'll be all right. But we can't take any chances, so Mommy and I have to take him back to the hospital. We'll bring him home again in a few days. Gramma's on her way back to be with you, and either Mommy or I will come home tomorrow night.

"But what about my birthday? Aren't we going to have a birthday party?"

I felt horrible. How to make all of this work? To love my daughter at the same time we were struggling to keep Tommy alive? There just was no easy answer.

"Shannon," I said, "I promise that you'll have a great birthday. It just can't be right now. Your mother and I love you very much, and we'll celebrate your birthday soon—but right now, we have to be a family and work together to make Tommy well. All of us have to help. Do you understand?"

I heard her sniffle and wipe her tears away.

"I'll pray for Tommy," my little girl said. "I'll pray all the time and very hard."

I hugged her, holding her close.

"I'll bet God really hears the prayers of special little children like you. That's even better than Tommy's medicine."

I wish I really believed that, I thought. But maybe, just maybe it was true.

Bridgette's mother arrived in an hour, and sometime around three in the morning, we drove a bundled-up Tommy back to the hospital he hated.

Not wanting to awaken Dr. Hennessy, we reached the resident on call and actually were pleased to learn that it was Dr. Edwards, the oncology fellow. Dr. Hennessy had told us that this young man had real talent, and I had immediately liked him when we met during the first round of chemo.

I told him what was going on with Tommy, and he said that they would be ready for us when we arrived.

Even though it was the middle of the night when we pulled up in front of the building, two orderlies were waiting, and Tommy was whisked inside while we parked the car. By the time we arrived in his room with our masks once again in place, Tommy was hooked up, and the meds were flowing. Our chance at a small window of normalcy was over, and we were once again captured by the routine that cancer imposed.

chapter 10

By the middle of the next day, Tommy seemed more settled, possibly because the meds pouring into his body had broken the fever and he was feeling better. A pattern seemed to be emerging. Just before the next round of chemo would begin, if you were lucky there would be a period of virtual normalcy. During this time the sores were better, the fever was broken, and the child's positive spirit would reemerge.

And so like all little boys, Tommy wanted to be active. All Children's Hospitals have a living room in the cancer wards, a place where kids could gain a respite from the burden of the disease and on good days spend time doing kid things. Dr. Hennessy allowed Tommy to have short periods out of his room with a mask in place but off the catheter and the medicine. On his first trip to the play area, I happened to be the parent on duty accompanying him down the hall.

Entering the room, I heard the *clang, beep,* and *pow* of some kind of video game being played. Right away, this got Tommy's attention.

"Dad," he said, "there's a little girl playing Mario Brothers on a Wii."

"Okay, good," I said, having no idea what he really meant. Video games had never been particularly important to a blind man, but I knew Tommy loved them. "Well," I said, "why don't you go talk to her? I'll just sit here and take a rest. Go ahead."

Tommy moved to where the little girl was seated in front of the screen. I heard him say, "Hi! Would you mind if I played with you?"

The little girl didn't answer, obviously intent on playing her game.

"Oh, no!" she said. "You made me lose! I fell in the pit and I can't get out."

"I'm sorry," Tommy said, "but you can start the game again."

"Maybe," she said. "You never know. I mean, if the plants eat you or the mushrooms get you or somebody in the underworld gets you—if you don't have enough coins to keep you safe, you lose the game."

Tommy said, "But it's a good game, even if you don't win."

"Yeah. I guess so," she replied pensively. "So you want to play?"

"Yeah," Tommy said. "What's your name?"

"Shaniqua Adams," she told him.

"Shaniqua," Tommy said. "That's a pretty name. I'm Tommy O'Connor."

"Thanks, Tommy," she responded shyly. "Let's play."

For the next three hours, the two children entertained each other, and I just sat quietly observing. Somewhere along the way, Shaniqua told Tommy that she had leukemia and that this was her third relapse. Tommy said he had a tumor in his arm, but he didn't know what kind of tumor it was.

As I listened to Shaniqua's intensity playing the game, I realized that this little child was somehow using Mario Brothers and the battle for safety as an allegory for her own life.

I had heard about how wise children could be, and I'd even experienced some of it with the stuff Tommy and Shannon had been saying since he got sick, but this little girl seemed to be an old soul. As she and Tommy talked as they played, she very rarely laughed out loud, yet I didn't feel that her face was frowning. Her voice had the sound of a smile in it, and I suppose that expressed her commitment to hope.

What I understood at the end of the three hours was that these two children, Tommy O'Connor and Shaniqua Adams, had become friends. And I figured that was really a good thing. By the time they returned to their rooms, they had exchanged cell phone numbers, and as Tommy struggled to eat some of his dinner, he and Shaniqua already had begun texting, a privilege I was happy to allow my son to continue.

The next morning the chemo started again, and this time the sores in Tommy's mouth were worse. We struggled with the fevers and then the predicted loss of hair. Out of Tommy's sight, Bridgette was in tears. Tommy always had beautiful blond curls—some of them Bridgette had even kept in a baby book—and now his hair was falling out in bunches.

When I asked him if he would rather shave his head, I was surprised to hear him say, "You mean like Shaniqua?"

"Oh, really?" I asked. "Did Shaniqua shave her head?"

"She's completely bald," Tommy said, "but she's still really pretty."

"Okay, pal," I laughed, "then let's have a shave-our-heads party. I'll do it with you."

"You don't have to do that, Dad," Tommy said. "You don't have cancer."

"I know," I told him, "but I want everybody to see how much I love my son, so if you're going to have a bald head, then I'll have one too."

A few days after the next round of chemo was completed, Bridgette became the hair stylist, helping to make a fashion statement for her two men.

That same day, Shaniqua came to visit Tommy in his room on her way home.

"I'm going home again," she said. "This time, I hope it's forever."

Bridgette and I were introduced to her mother and father, a couple delighted to be taking their daughter out of the hospital.

"These two have really become good friends," I said.

"Yes, they have," Mr. Adams agreed, "and it's been wonderful. I think we'll have to get them together when Tommy's out of here and back home."

We all agreed, and it was terrific to look forward to that possibility.

Finally, after twelve weeks of chemo rotations, Tommy was once again run through the battery of scans, and Dr. Hennessy told us that as soon as the results were in we would meet with Dr. Erickson to discuss the surgical options for the tumor.

I was beginning to feel the pressure of our circumstance rising to the breaking point. True, my boss in the DA office had given me as much latitude as he could, but it was painfully clear to both Bridgette and me that, since I had used up all my paid vacation along with my sick days, very soon we would be using up all of our savings. And what then? I didn't know. But I realized that was a problem I couldn't handle right now.

What I needed to deal with was that over the weeks of Tommy's therapy, I hadn't even been considering the surgery and the reality that two options existed: one, to salvage Tommy's arm; and the other, an idea almost unthinkable, to remove it. But now it hit me right in the gut.

Remove my son's arm? I couldn't even comprehend it. Oddly, my mind went to the absurd idea that this just couldn't happen because Tommy was a right-handed pitcher in Little League. Didn't everybody know that? Didn't they know how important your right arm is when you play baseball?

Bridgette was more practical. "Listen," she said, "whatever we have to do to save our son is what we're going to do. Have you noticed over the weeks that he's become much better using his left hand? He even handles a knife and fork pretty well. Kids are very adaptable," she told me. But I heard her voice quaver and knew she was just as affected as I was.

"Okay," I told her, "but let's believe that it's option one—salvage."

Once again, we were in the conference room sitting opposite the two doctors who held Tommy's future in their hands.

Dr. Erickson led off. "Well, Mr. and Mrs. O'Connor," he said, "I'm very pleased to tell you that the tumor has shrunk considerably. As you know, we've been scanning Tommy throughout these weeks, and for a while it seemed to be touch-and-go as far as the tumor was concerned, but we are very sure that our margins have become appropriate to perform limb salvage surgery."

Our sighs were audible in the room, and both doctors heard

them. Bridgette was reaching for a Kleenex, and I fumbled in my sports coat pocket for a handkerchief.

Dr. Hennessy took up the conversation. "We're also very pleased to tell you that all of the tests indicate that at this point, the cancer is confined to the site, Tommy's upper arm."

Dr. Erickson went on. "Here's how we'll approach the surgery. First, we'll take out any part of Tommy's bone in which we have found tumor, along with an appropriate margin to guarantee the integrity of the site. My best guess is that we will remove about two-thirds of Tommy's humerus and replace it with a prosthetic."

"Wow," I said. "That seems like an awful lot."

"It is," Dr. Erickson agreed. And then he added gently, "But you understand that it's much better than the alternative."

"Of course," Bridgette said, "and I know that the body accepts prosthetics quite well."

"Yes, it does. We've had great results with these kinds of prosthetics, and I know from my time with Tommy that he's a little boy with a winning attitude."

I smiled thinking about that. "He's a winner, all right," I said proudly.

Dr. Erickson continued, "You need to understand that this is a very painful surgery and that there is a great deal of rehabilitation involved. Tommy will not only have to endure physical therapy on his arm, but he also will continue his chemo regimen after some appropriate rest and recovery."

"How do we determine how long he needs to be on chemo and radiation treatments?" Bridgette asked.

"It's really medical instinct," Dr. Hennessy said. "We look at the success protocols of other patients and continue to scan Tommy and then take our best guess. But my thinking is that

Tommy's therapy protocol will be anywhere from six to eight more months. Like Dr. Erickson said, Mr. and Mrs. O'Connor, this is not easy. Tommy still has to face a lot before we can declare him cancer-free."

Bridgette's sigh was audible as the enormity of what we were facing weighted us down, consumed us, became overwhelming.

Cancer-free. The words were like blue sky to a blind man. Like the brightest possible rainbow, a magnificent sunset, or a beautiful watercolor. Cancer-free. Was it possible?

"Doctor?" I asked, not able to stop my smile, "are you telling us that Tommy's chances are greatly improved?"

Dr. Hennessy was very careful. "What we know right now, Mr. O'Connor, is that the tumor has shrunk considerably. There is no metastasis, and we will be able to perform limb salvage. I don't think it's appropriate to say that we have an understanding that suggests Tommy's chances have improved. Remember, he will be returning to a chemo regimen after about a month at home following surgery."

I couldn't help myself. "Yeah, but a month at home is going to be great. Great for Tommy and for all of us."

Dr. Hennessy was still being circumspect. "I'm sure it will, but remember what Dr. Erickson said. This surgery is painful, and the connected physical therapy is difficult too. We're putting an artificial bone in place, and that involves muscle, tendons, and ligaments. Right now, we don't know how much of that other tissue Dr. Erickson will have to affect when he performs the surgery, so assessing Tommy's mobility is impossible."

"Well," Bridgette said, "I'm sure you're right, Dr. Hennessy, but a lot can be achieved in a loving setting. I don't mean to suggest that the hospital hasn't been great. In fact, the staff here at Dana-Farber has been magnificent. But there's nothing like home."

"You're right," Dr. Hennessy said, smiling. "There is nothing like home."

"How much should we tell Tommy?" I asked.

"Well," Dr. Erickson put in, "from my experience this is the time when you want to be very positive. Tommy's going to have surgery to get back the use of his arm. That's how I'd say it to your son. And he's going to be home for a while."

Dr. Hennessy was still being careful. "I think Tommy will probably ask you if his cancer is gone."

"What should we tell him?" Bridgette asked.

"I suggest you tell Tommy that we're making great progress and that we're beating the disease, but that he will have to undergo chemotherapy again. He's not going to like that, but I don't think it's ever appropriate to hide that information from a child. They mature pretty quickly when they have cancer. It's as if their understanding expands by years."

"I've noticed that," Bridgette said. "The way Tommy asks questions now—it's as if he has grown up overnight."

"Yes, but the best things he has going for him, Mrs. O'Connor, are the love of your family and his own positive attitude. Children seem to be able to shake off adversity better than we can and they always keep trying."

"Okay," I said. "When would you suggest performing the surgery?"

Dr. Erickson punched up his calendar on his computer screen.

"Let's see," he said. "This is Tuesday, right? And I think we can clear an operating theater on Friday morning at, let's see, eight o'clock. Is that okay with everyone?"

"That'll be fine," Bridgette said. "We'll tell Tommy tonight at dinner."

"Good," Dr. Erickson said, sounding positive. "Even though Tommy has been uncomfortable, this might be a night when food could taste pretty good."

And it did.

An hour later we had explained to Tommy what was going to happen, and for the first time since the onset of his cancer, our son seemed genuinely excited. Even though we were honest and told him that surgery would be painful and that he would have to return to chemo, what seemed to be centered in our little boy's mind was the idea that he would be going home. Back to Scituate. Back to his family. Home.

And temporarily, I guess Bridgette and I were feeling the same way. The idea, the feeling, the word remained front and center in our minds. *Home.*

chapter 11

Time seemed to be moving at different speeds surrounding Tommy's illness. When he felt good, time moved too fast; yet when he was in agony, time dragged as his pain increased. In those moments, I would sit, unable to help, unable to heal, unable to make a difference; and this sense of my own inadequacy was devastating. And so hours continued to crawl as Bridgette and I sat in the waiting room while Dr. Erickson worked to salvage Tommy's arm.

Bridgette and I didn't speak much during the surgery. That was probably part of what made time seem to move so slowly, but there wasn't much to say. We were both emotionally exhausted, wanting only to have the operation over with and bring our little boy home. I dozed in my chair, surprised that sleep could happen when we were under this kind of tension—but remembering that as a high school athlete I often dozed off before a wrestling match because the nerves were too much to handle. It was in one of these drowsy states that I felt Bridgette tap me on the shoulder as Dr. Erickson came into the room.

"Mr. and Mrs. O'Connor," he said, smiling, "Tommy's surgery couldn't have gone any better. The attachment of muscle, ligaments, and tendons was not compromised by the tumor, and I was also very pleased to find that the nerves have not been damaged. I'm not suggesting that Tommy will pitch in the big leagues, but I do expect that he will have excellent use of his arm following extensive physical therapy.

"However, let me remind you that this surgery was complicated, and your son will experience a great deal of pain during the healing process. Dr. Hennessy will want to talk to you about pain management and the effective course of treatment, but for today I'm very pleased to say that the surgical outcome is extremely positive."

It didn't seem so positive when Tommy was back in his room following the operation. He was heavily medicated for the pain, and even though we were full of happiness and a sense of relief, our son was continuing to suffer.

What to think at that moment? I was afraid to allow hope because the weight of disappointment was more than I believed I could handle. I was aware of my own fragile humanity, and though I was giving the impression of paternal strength, my psyche was as fragile as a cloud suspended until reality defined its future.

Dr. Hennessy asked us to join her for a consultation the next afternoon to discuss Tommy's overall situation. I wasn't sure what that meant, but over the weeks I had come to trust Jennifer Hennessy, and we had just received such a positive report from Dr. Erickson, so I entered the meeting with little trepidation.

I was taken back when I sensed that there were a number of

people in the room. *Isn't this supposed to be a private matter? I thought. A consultation between physician and family?*

Maybe my face showed my concern because Dr. Hennessy began right away. "Mr. and Mrs. O'Connor," she said, "I want you to meet members of our palliative care team."

I heard Bridgette's intake of breath. "Palliative!" she exclaimed. "In my experience as a practicing nurse, people talk about palliative care as a way to manage"—she nearly choked on the words—"death and dying. Tommy's not dying. He's not."

Dr. Hennessy got up from her chair and came around the conference table to sit next to Bridgette. "No, no, Mrs. O'Connor. Palliative care is about much, much more than end-of-life. It's about pain management, counseling, and all other outside supports away from the hospital, including spiritual well-being. You know, the Greeks have a word for it that I think is very appropriate. They say *holisthia,* meaning the whole patient—mind, soul, heart, and body. That's the concept that I think it's important to understand when we talk about palliative care."

I felt Bridgette relax beside me.

"Our team is here to help you with every aspect of Tommy's health and well-being. So let me describe what the members of our team do, and then maybe you'll understand a little better.

"First we have a social services director who is here to help you with the emotional issues you're facing. Then we have an outpatient oncology nurse who will help you manage the pain meds I will be prescribing.

"I probably should have told you," added Dr. Hennessy, "that I'm not only a pediatric oncologist, but I'm also a palliative care physician. I guess"—she smiled—"you're getting two for the price of one. We're very proud of what we do here at Farber in terms of the way we organize our case management.

"And finally, let me introduce you to the third member of our team. This is our spiritual director, Rev. Clayton McRae. He's also our resident marathon runner and gourmet chef."

The man's laugh was deep and rich. In my experience, people laugh in different ways and with different sounds. We've all heard the *he-he*'s or *ha-ha*'s or *ho-ho*'s in different pitches and registers, but when the laugh is open and rich, its sound doesn't really matter as much as its feeling. And when Rev. McRae laughed, my instinct said, *I bet I'll like him.*

"Mr. and Mrs. O'Connor," he said, his Texas accent offered as a contrast to the way the rest of us spoke, "Dr. Hennessy is much too kind. I'm really an addictive person. I'm addicted to good food, whether I cook it or someone else does, and so I run marathons so that I don't become a fat hospital chaplain."

Dr. Hennessy added again, "You're not being fair, Clayton. You also run marathons and raise a great deal of money for Farber. He heads our run-for-cancer group that does the Boston marathon every year. How many runners did you have last April?" she asked.

"Our contingent was rather substantial," he said, smiling. "I think our numbers were well over five hundred, and we raised a little over a hundred thousand dollars, not bad if I do say so myself. You both look very fit. Do either of you run?"

"I do," I said, "with my friend Bailey here."

"Ah," he said. "It's good to have a dog to drag you uphill when you're a little tired."

Now I laughed, realizing I really did like this man. "He is pretty strong," I said, "but I don't think he could run a marathon."

"What about you?" Rev. McRae asked. "Is there a marathon in your future? Sorry," he added quickly. "This isn't the time for a sales pitch. We'll talk about that on another day."

He continued, "I want to tell you that I understand spirituality is a very personal matter and that people's faith is clearly their own business. I happen to be Presbyterian, but I don't really have much interest in denominations. What I think matters is whether or not a family believes that God has a role to play in the health of their children and in their own lives. I'm here to help you examine that question or help you reinforce what may be already your personal faith. So, please call on me, as a member of this team, if I can be of any help. And like my partners have said, we are a twenty-four/seven group."

"Thank you, Rev. McRae," Dr. Hennessy said. "I hope you can see that you're in a room of people committed to Tommy's well-being and to that of your family. You all are truly our team's major concern, and we are absolutely committed to working with you at every stage of Tommy's care."

Following the meeting, Bridgette and I shared a bad cup of coffee in the hospital cafeteria.

"So, what did you think of the palliative care team?" I asked.

"Very impressive," she said. "When you're a nurse, you learn to read people's competence very quickly. When I worked in surgery, I could tell immediately what kind of doctor I'd be dealing with during a procedure, and it was important to be able to understand the person who would be holding the scalpel. What I felt about the team was that they were competent and committed, and they know that's exactly what we want for Tommy. I did get a scare when I heard the term *palliative care*, because I didn't really understand its scope."

"What's the difference between hospice and palliative care?" I asked.

"First of all," she said, "palliative is an outpatient service, whereas much of what hospice does is involved in the hospital. Second, I get the impression that there's a lot more interest in the holistic side of patient involvement from this team, and I love the idea that they're talking about treating all of us—the whole family."

"Okay," I said. "How about the chaplain, the spiritual director? Did you feel he might be a Bible thumper?"

"You mean because he was from the South?" Bridgette asked.

"I don't know. You know faith hasn't been a big part of my life."

"What I felt about him," she said, "at least in this initial meeting, was that he is a very spiritual man with well-honed human skill to go along with it."

"I think I agree with you," I said. "My instinct was that I liked him a lot. I don't know how much he'll have to do with Tommy and us, but I'm glad he's on the team."

"Okay," she said, rising. "Let me walk you downstairs and send you on your way home to Shannon. I'm so excited that in just a few more days we'll be back in our own house, and we'll be a family living together again, even if it's just for a little while."

I reached across the table and took her hand. "We're always a family. No matter where we are."

Later that night, after tucking Shannon in, I sat outside on our deck with Bailey at my feet, trying to get a handle on my feelings. Tommy was coming home. That thought was central in my head. But then he would be returning to the hospital for more chemo, which meant that the medical team was still concerned—very concerned, as Dr. Hennessy had said—about cancer.

So what was I supposed to think? I decided that I needed to look at Tommy's homecoming as a respite, a chance for all of us to gather our strength, to gain some balance, to prepare. *Prepare for what?* I wondered. Prepare to be the best support system for Tommy possible. In that moment in the dark, I realized that the battle for Tommy's life centered on Tommy, not what we thought or what the doctors believed they could do for him, but what he felt, what he believed, how he chose to fight. He might be only eleven, but this thing in his system, this cancer, was in the most direct sense his personal enemy, his disease, his cellular curse.

I shook my head, angry, so full of doubts. If the palliative care team would be there 24/7, I committed that I would compete against this disease in the very same way.

chapter 12

With Tommy getting ready to come home for somewhere between four and six weeks, I knew that I had to go back to work. The District Attorney, Joseph Martelli, had let me keep my job over the past few months without even putting me on extended leave and continued to pay me. It was now time for me to pay him back by doing some real work.

Arriving at my office, I was extremely touched by the greeting I got from my colleagues and staff. Their compassion was genuine, I could tell. The people were heartfelt in the way they reached out to me. Everyone wanted to know how Tommy was doing, and many of them told me that our whole family had been in their prayers.

The prayer thing again, I thought. Well, I didn't know how much good it did, but if God was listening, Tommy's case for mercy was certainly being well presented.

Joseph Martelli was a fast-talking, no-nonsense, East Boston Italian. Somehow, even on a public servant's salary, he was always dapper. He told me that there were tailors in his family, and based on his suits—the way my coworkers described them—I believed him. Impatient and brilliant but with a heart that was truly Sicilian in its dynamic emotions, Martelli had always been great for me to work for, and today was no exception.

"So here's what we're gonna do, O'Connor. I'm not going to give you a specific caseload. I'm going to ask you to work directly for me and coordinate counsel. Make sure everyone's moving along appropriately."

"Don't we have people for that, Joe?" I asked.

"Operationally, that's true, but what I'm really talking about is case strategy. With all the crap I have to do up there on Beacon Hill to keep the politicians happy, I'm not able to provide any of our people with the right kind of mentoring. You know, the way I mentored you. Remember? I took a dumb Irishman who was—and excuse my insensitivity—handicapped and made you a superstar."

I laughed.

"I don't think you got that quite right, boss. I actually think I made you look pretty good."

We both laughed.

"Okay," he went on, "when you come in on Monday I'll have a briefing prepared for you on everything that's pending around here. Then you can set up conference schedules with all the teams and create a status board. Okay?"

"All right," I said. "This'll be fun."

"Just remember," the DA went on, "this is temporary. As soon as Tommy is healthy enough, you're going to be right back in the courtroom, using that blind stuff of yours to get some sympathy from juries and putting bad guys where they belong."

We shook hands, and Bailey and I grabbed a cab to the hospital.

* * *

Bridgette met me in the lobby.

"Hey," she said. "Tommy's sleeping, and I asked the duty nurse to tell him that we've gone out for some lunch when he wakes up. How would you feel about getting me out of here for a while and having a real meal?"

"Great idea," I said. "Where would you like to go?"

"Legal Seafood," she said. "I'm dying for some lobster."

"An excellent choice. Let's go."

Ten minutes later we were sitting opposite each other at a lovely corner table, trying to decide what we should have beyond the lobster from the extensive menu.

With Tommy coming home, we did something decadent and each had a glass of wine, toasting our family getting back together as one, even if it was only for a little while.

Bridgette said that she had been searching out some physical therapists who could begin Tommy's rehabilitation closer to Scituate.

"There are three," she said. "Two at South Shore Hospital in Braintree and one outsource clinic in Quincy that everybody at Children's feels good about."

"Okay," I said. "That will make the process a lot easier than having to drive downtown. What else have you been doing with your morning?"

"Well, I had a long conversation with the social worker about the kinds of things Social Services offers to Tommy. We think we know a lot about how to talk to kids just because we have them, but as I listened to her I realized that there really is a technique to these kinds of difficult discussions that parents don't always understand."

"I think that's probably because parents love their children so much that it's almost impossible to be objective."

"That's right," Bridgette said, "but there's also a specific way of dialoguing that comes out of experience and skill sets. I got the feeling that the most important part of what she hoped to achieve with Tommy would be exploring and soothing his fears. Finding out what he's afraid of, what he's really thinking. Even though he loves us, I'm not sure that any child would express these things to a parent. Tommy wouldn't want to upset us. Sometimes talking to a sensitive stranger is easier."

"I get it," I told her. "I'm always amazed at how witnesses talk to me. It's as if because I'm blind there's a screen up between us."

Bridgette smiled. "Kind of like going to confession at church, right?"

"Well," I said, smiling myself, "if you have any sins to confess, little girl, please go right ahead. I'm more than prepared to listen. Seriously, I think you're right. I'm glad that Social Services will be talking directly to Tommy, and I'm pleased that the whole palliative team is in place to help us with every aspect of his illness, especially pain management."

Bridgette took a long drink of her chardonnay. "I also spent quite a bit of time with the chaplain, Rev. McRae."

"I bet that was informative," I said, leaning back in my chair.

"There you go, leaning back like that as if you're moving away from any conversation about God. Listen, Brian," she continued, "before I met you I prayed the prayer that's common to every young woman—that someone special would come into my life, be my lover, be my husband, and voila! God brought me you. Then I asked to have a wonderful family, and voila! We got Tommy and Shannon."

The words were out before I could close them off.

"Yeah, and now Tommy has cancer, so how's that working for you?"

Bridgette leaned across the table, and I could feel her eyes boring right through me.

"That's not fair," she said. "God didn't cause Tommy's cancer. Genetics or biology made that happen. But I believe God can help us through this, and I believe in the power of prayer, and I'll tell you what else: I believe you should be talking to Rev. McRae, because if this thing gets worse, we're all going to need the support of something stronger than medicine."

In our thirteen years of marriage, Bridgette had never spoken to me this way. Most the time when we disagreed, it didn't become emotional because our trust and our love ran so deep. But here, in the middle of this busy restaurant, the full power of her feelings impacted me. I realized that I not only had to take her seriously, but I also had to become her true partner in this process.

"All right," I said. "I'll talk to him. And I'll try to be open-minded about what he has to say."

Bridgette took my hand, softening. "Look, Brian, I have a feeling that because of your blindness and because of the loneliness you experienced as a child, you became very self-sufficient, used to relying only on yourself."

"I suppose that's true," I said. "I haven't really thought about it."

"Then I came into your life, and then we had Shannon and Tommy. A few years ago you got Bailey. So for the first time you shared your life with an animal and people you decided to trust. So Tommy's sick and you're angry, and I feel that you're retreating into yourself, putting up those barriers you think will help you survive whatever we're going to have to face. I want you to consider ideas that are outside yourself, maybe even larger than yourself—ideas that can help you get through whatever course this disease takes."

"Bridgette," I said earnestly, "you keep saying things like 'whatever course it takes.' I don't think that's the right attitude to have. We should commit to believing that together we're going to beat this thing."

Bridgette was quiet as the seconds ticked by, and then she said, "We don't know what God has in mind for Tommy, Brian. We just don't know."

I wanted to argue with her, but I bit my lip. I had tried to ignore the fact that even after Dr. Erickson's successful surgery, cancer was still a foe.

"Okay," I said. "I'll talk to Rev. McRae. I promise. In fact, I'll call to set up an appointment with him right now."

We paid the check and headed back to the hospital.

I opened my cell phone and dialed his number, which I had stored there, along with those of the other team members.

"Hello. This is Clayton McRae."

"Rev. McRae, it's Brian O'Connor, Tommy's father. My wife suggested that you might have a few minutes to talk with me."

"Sure," he said. "When would you like to talk, Mr. O'Connor?"

"Oh, whenever it's convenient."

"Where are you right now?"

"On my way back to the hospital," he said.

"Well, then meet me in the cafeteria for some of our bad hospital coffee."

I wasn't ready for that immediate response, but with Bridgette right next to me, I was trapped.

"Okay," I said. "I'll meet you there in about twenty minutes."

When I hung up, Bridgette said, "Thank you, Brian. I really believe Rev. McRae can be helpful. I'll go upstairs and see how Tommy's doing while you two talk."

"All right," I said. "I'll see you in a little while."

* * *

Bailey had just settled down under the table when Rev. McRae seemed to bound into the room. I heard the sound of his running shoes as he rapidly crossed the cafeteria. I stood, and we shook hands. His grip seemed as warm as his laugh, firm but not threatening. McRae was a moderate pumper, his handshake telling me that he was glad to be here but classy enough not to be too overt.

Both of us poured a cup of coffee, adding milk and sugar to reduce the acid that could eat away at our stomachs, and sat down.

"I'm glad you called," McRae said, opening the conversation. "I meant it when I told you and Mrs. O'Connor that I was here for you twenty-four/seven. So I'm delighted that you're giving me the opportunity to be helpful to your family. Conversations about spiritual matters are always hard to begin. Do you have any questions I might help with?"

I laughed. "No, not really," I said, being honest. "You see, faith, I mean, God hasn't been a big part of my life. My wife says it's because of my being blind. She believes I became so self-sufficient that I stopped relying on anyone or anything, including—well, God."

McRae leaned back in his chair, and I could hear him rock, tilting the legs off the ground.

"I think I understand," he said. "Believing may seem easy to some people, but the leap of faith required to really bring God into your life is not necessarily easy, and there certainly isn't a universal formula to make it happen. For some people, the process of prayer and reading the Word gets them where they need to go; but for others, it's life experience that humbles us enough to believe there must be something greater than ourselves. One thing I'm sure of: no one can define the absolutes that draw people to Christ.

"My job is to help people explore the mystery of faith and to expose them to God's Word with, hopefully, some appropriate interpretation that helps them in their need. I think the reason some of us go on and acquire a doctorate in theology is because in some ways we believe that we're doctors of the soul, and our most powerful medicine is the Word of God."

"I have to admit, I haven't even read the Bible," I said. "I mean, growing up Catholic I took religious education, and my mother made sure I went to Mass and confession. But frankly it was always just something I had to do, not something I committed to or took much interest in."

Rev. McRae smiled. "That's okay," he said. "God's always waiting for you, always holding out His hand and wanting you to take it. Right up to the last day of your earthly life, God is hoping that you'll embrace Him. I really believe that. And just so you know, my calling to the ministry came very late."

"Oh, did you have something else that you wanted to be?" I asked.

"Yeah," he chuckled. "I wanted to be Jimi Hendrix. I play pretty good guitar, if I do say so myself, and I worked in bands all through high school and college until I went on to seminary."

"Wow," I said. "Was there a turning point? I mean, a moment when you felt—what is it—the calling?"

"I suppose it was always there," he told me. "That's what God's Word really is about. It's always present if we're willing to listen. I just wasn't willing to hear Him until my junior year in college, when I spent the summer on an Indian reservation in Arizona working with Navajo kids. Then I realized that playing rock and roll didn't seem particularly valuable. Once I understood that, the calling to God's service sounded loud and clear in my head. I realized I couldn't live for myself any longer, so I gave my life to Christ. I enrolled in divinity school, and here I am."

"Where do you live?" I asked.

"South of Boston in Cohasset."

"Really? Then we're almost neighbors."

"Oh?" he said, surprised. "Where do you live?"

"In Scituate."

"Just the next town," he noted, taking a sip of his coffee.

"Do you commute by ferry?" I asked.

"All the time. It's a great way to get to Boston. The boats are never slow, even in the middle of winter."

"I have a driver," I told him, "but I have used the boat. Maybe I ought to try it more often."

"Sure. You can just get a cab to your office right from the dock. It would probably be a lot faster."

"Good suggestion. Thanks for the tip," I said.

"By the way, you mentioned you're a runner. Maybe we could share some jogging and a little contemplative conversation along the way. Have you run with other people before?"

"A few times." I thought about Bailey at my feet. "Well, it would certainly be a way for me to add some extra miles without putting pressure on the big dog." I was surprised at what I said next. "The doctor told us we're going to bring Tommy home early next week, and once we get him settled, I really would enjoy sharing some morning runs around the lighthouse, if that works with your schedule. Thanks for bringing it up."

Why did I tell him that? I wondered. Why had I allowed myself to be taken in by this man with an easy Texas style, who didn't seem to be imposing God on me, but—what—was allowing me talk about God in my own way? I wasn't sure, but I'd already crossed the line.

"Terrific," Rev. McRae said, the enthusiasm obvious in his voice. "The road can get pretty lonely early in the morning. There are times when solo contemplation is a good idea, but I'm a social animal, so don't think that our talk will just be about God. I'm open to conversation about politics, sports, or anything else that might come up along the way. Are you planning to go upstairs to be with Tommy?"

"Yes," I said. "That's what I had in mind."

"Well," he said, "why don't you just have that big dog of yours walk along on leash and take my arm to give me a chance to practice guiding? I know Bailey's a lot better than I'll ever be, but if we're going to run together, I ought to get used to the process, don't you think?"

I'm about six-three, and when I took Rev. McRae's arm it seemed to me we were the same height, though he was thinner, probably in much better shape.

As we worked our way out of the cafeteria, I only hit my knee once on the edge of a table.

"I'm sorry," he said. "I'm just not used to having to provide more than me with space."

"Happens to me all the time," I chuckled. "That's why I usually let Bailey do the job."

"I'll get better," he said. "I promise."

By the time we rode up the elevator and arrived at Tommy's room, I was back to feeling at ease with this guy. Maybe it was possible for me to make a new friend, and I had to admit that there was something intriguing about exploring the possibility of God in my life. The realist in me said anything that would make dealing with Tommy's cancer easier should be examined, and if that meant spending some time with this good man, why not take a chance?

chapter 13

Tommy's homecoming was not what we expected, but then again, I don't know what we expected. Somehow in my head the idea that there was currently no cancer to be found anywhere in his system made everything else pale by comparison, yet the surgeon, Dr. Erickson, had made it clear that there would be major postsurgical complications to deal with and that our son would be in a great deal of pain.

Though the palliative care people were doing their best to mitigate Tommy's suffering, the bottom line was that it was awful. The first five nights that he was home Bridgette and I alternated shifts, sitting at the side of his bed, talking to him, rubbing his back, and doing everything we could to console our little boy.

At some points when the meds were wearing off, Tommy would moan in discomfort, and we would try to talk to him positively about how great he would feel after his arm had healed. Even with Tommy's optimism, the pain limited any thoughts our son might have had about being well again.

I don't think there's a worse moment for a parent than watching your child suffer, especially when there is very little you can do about it. On the third night, at maybe one or two in the morning, Tommy was awake and in a lot of pain.

I heard him turn his head on the pillow and ask, "Dad, why is this happening to me? The cancer? The surgery? Everything? I've asked God but I can't seem to get an answer."

At that moment, I wished Bridgette had been with him and not me. Through her faith she might have had an answer, but I did not.

All I could say was, "I don't know, Tommy. I really don't know, but we'll get through this. Next year, you'll be back out there pitching."

"Dad, I've been thinking about that. As soon as I feel good enough, I'm thinking I should start to learn to use my left arm to pitch. Maybe I can learn to do it as a southpaw."

Wow, I thought. *The optimism of children.*

"I suppose that's possible," I said, glad to have the diversion of a late-night conversation. "You know, Tommy, there are a lot of golfers who are left-handed but they learn to play the game right-handed so that their left arm, the lead arm, will be stronger hitting the ball. Some of these guys say that they're even better playing that way. I suppose it would take us a while to get your left arm strong enough and teach you the motion, but you know what? That's something for a father and son to look forward to. And anyway there aren't as many good left-handers in the big leagues, so there wouldn't be as much competition."

I had a memory flash. "You know, pal, a few years ago there was a guy in the majors named Jim Abbott. He pitched for the L.A. Angels. This guy had only one arm."

"One arm?" Tommy said, through his pain. "How did he do it?"

"I don't know exactly," I said, "but somehow he was able to

throw the ball and get the glove back on his hand in time to catch it if someone hit it back to the pitcher or when the catcher threw it back to the mound. It was really amazing. Also, way back in the 1930s, there was a pitcher named Monty Stratton. They made a movie about his life, with the famous actor Jimmy Stewart playing the part. Monty lost his leg in a hunting accident but worked his way back to the big leagues and I think actually won a few games."

I reached over and began to rub my son's back.

"You see, Tommy, anything is possible if you believe hard enough. When I was a little boy about your age, everybody said there were many things that I couldn't do because I was blind, but you know, somehow you find a way."

"Okay, Dad," Tommy said, finally sounding sleepy. "I guess we'll just have to find a way. 'Cause I'll never give up baseball."

Almost unable to contain my emotions, I leaned over and kissed Tommy on the cheek.

"You bet, pal," I said. "We'll just have to find a way."

It was Saturday morning. I remember that because the night before was the first night Bridgette and I had a reasonable night's sleep since Tommy had come home. The phone rang as we were having our first cup of coffee, and the voice on the other end was just too ebullient.

"Good morning," Rev. McRae said. "What a beautiful fall morning it is for two guys to put on their running shoes and have a chat."

What is he talking about? I thought. *Fall? Was it really?*

And then I remembered. Throughout the summer we had been in the hospital. We had never gone to the beach or put our feet in the ocean. Summer had flown by, and we had missed it.

"Okay," I said, "but I just woke up. How about in an hour?"

"That'd be fine," he said. "Nine o'clock. Have your running shoes on."

I put the phone down but didn't move, thinking about how time had lost meaning. Time was about Tommy, and that made me remember that I'd better begin to pay attention to a little girl sleeping upstairs. *Siblings get the short end of the stick when a child is this sick,* I thought. *We really need to do something special for Shannon.*

McRae showed up right on time, and I met him outside the house. I took in a big gulp of air. "Wow," I said, "what an incredible morning! Spring and fall are the times when the potpourri of smells is at its best with the ocean our constant."

"Feeling poetic this morning?" he said, laughing softly.

"Oh, sorry. No. It's just . . . well, over the last few months I haven't been paying much attention to the senses."

"But they mean a lot to you. Right?"

"Everything," I said. "The four of them. They're my eyes on the world. I've been trying to teach my children to plug in all their senses because I think they could learn a lot more about life if they did, and they'd certainly come to appreciate their surroundings more."

"Well, then, you can sharpen my senses when we're on the run. I'm embarrassed to say I don't use them very well either. I suppose I'm too sight-dependent."

"Okay," I said. "But if we're going to become running partners, I'm kind of glad you use your eyes well—so that I don't trip or something."

"How do we do this?" he asked. "I know with your dog you've got a harness and leash, but I don't think it would be good for either of our reputations if I wore that stuff."

"No," I laughed, "but I kind of like the picture. I think what we'll do in the beginning is have me take your arm until you get used to telling me to pick my feet up when there's ruts in the road or move in closer to you when traffic is coming or when we have to step up and down a curb. You'll get the idea. All you really have to do is watch Bridgette when we're together. She's seamless. Actually, she's even better than Bailey."

Right at that moment I heard the big dog whining from inside.

"Bailey knows I've got my running shoes on," I told the minister. "I suppose he doesn't understand why he's not going."

"Sorry, Bailey," McRae yelled. "You go most of the other days. We'd better get started," he said, "before I feel any guiltier about Bailey."

I took his arm, and we began our maiden voyage—running toward what? Friendship? Understanding?

As we rounded the lighthouse on my usual morning course, I asked Rev. McRae the first of the questions that were weighing heavy on my mind. "So what's your angle?" I asked. "Are you one of those Bible-thumping fundamentalists, trying to convert me to your denomination?"

McRae chuckled. "No, no. I'm just a sinner who found a Savior, that's all. Like I told you when we met, as a hospital chaplain, I don't hold to one denomination over another. I just explain God the best I know how and minister to people wherever needed."

I nodded, grateful for his honesty. I decided to return the favor. "Okay, here's the deal. I told you the other day that I'm at best an agnostic. Bridgette says that it's because of my blindness.

She believes that I never really learned to rely on anyone for anything."

"That's a pretty lonely way to live," McRae commented. "What changed it?"

"My family. Bridgette particularly, my children, and now Bailey. I've learned that I'll never truly be independent. What I tell people is that we're *all* interdependent. It sure makes life a lot easier."

My point was emphasized as I nearly tripped over a tree branch that had been blown down the night before.

"Sorry," Clayton said. "I've really got to pay attention to your feet."

I shrugged it off. "Hey," I said lightly, "it's not easy to avoid bumps in the road when the guy you're guiding has size fourteens. But let me go on. I just never really brought God into my life. It wasn't that I was in denial. I just . . . well, I wasn't moved."

"By the Holy Spirit," he said. "To be one. Whole," he emphasized the word. "Whole with God. Here comes a rut in the road. Pick up your feet."

"Good job," I said. "You're getting the idea real quick."

"You're a lawyer," he said. "I don't want any lawsuits."

"I'm a criminal attorney," I said, smiling. "That's a civil issue. Anyway, the question still stands. Why are you so sure that there is a God?"

"Why are you so sure there isn't?"

"Okay, good point. But doesn't that make us all doubters? I mean, aren't you kind of a doubting Clayton?"

"Some days, yes, I guess that's right; but on the days when I struggle with my faith, I choose to believe that there are other people believing for me and that history is on my side, and it's all true."

"So what are we talking about here? A daisy chain of Christians?" I asked. "Is God an absolute, or is faith just people who mentor people to keep alive their basic hope of an afterlife?"

"Let me tell you something politely, my new friend," he said. "What you're expressing is really arrogant. It sounds like the apostle Thomas when he told the others that he wanted to put his fingers on Jesus' hands and feet where the nails had penetrated and wanted to touch the wound in His side. Is that what you think you need? I choose to believe that there's something bigger than me that created the universe. Even scientists can't really break that down and refute the possibility of"—and he used the word strongly—"God.

"Look, I have days when I'm a little cloudy and confused or I'm angry and upset. That's when I turn to someone else's faith to inspire me, and then my personal storm passes, and I remind myself that I believe—and it's been the truth all along—there is a God.

"I'll tell you something else. You know, God doesn't need my belief or my unbelief to be true. The bottom line is that I'm not that important. I'm loved, but my occasional anger at God or my disappointment, my sin, my doubt doesn't diminish God. Think of the times when your kids get upset, and they even say things like 'Dad, I hate you.'"

"Well, that hasn't happened to me yet," I said.

"Oh, it will," he said knowingly. "You can count on it. At the time it happens you don't really believe they hate you. You know they love you. You're going to trust that your love for your children will transcend whatever momentary upset they're in. That's how I believe in God. So if you're a bit of an agnostic, wouldn't it be easier for you to invest, to trust that there is someone larger than yourself out there who loves you?"

"I'm still learning about love," I said. And then I mumbled under my breath again, "I'm still learning."

"Listen," McRae pressed, "I understand your need for proof, but frankly I think you're wasting time. What you need to do is start to ask God for positive experiences that reveal His presence in your life, like our run this morning. Tell me why this is special."

"The senses," I answered without hesitation.

"Go on."

"Well," I said, "the blending of what you can smell this morning. There's the smell of dry leaves and a crispness in the air. I hear the sound of the waves in the distance. There are many different kinds of waves, you know, if you just learn to listen. Can you hear the bell buoy out there at the end of the bay? It's saying that it's going to be a beautiful morning. No storm on the horizon. And wow, can you hear the kids from the school down the hill?"

"No," he said. "They're too far away."

"Well, open your ears," I chuckled. "Just learn to listen."

"Okay," he said, "but right now pick up your feet. There's a speed bump coming."

"Thank you. You're getting it!"

"Okay, so aren't we saying that you have awareness, call it 'gifts of sensory skill,' that I don't have?"

"I guess so," I agreed.

"If that's true, shouldn't you be grateful, and isn't it possible that a power beyond you provided those special gifts?"

"Maybe," I said.

"Then isn't it also appropriate that you should be saying thank you? And that, my friend, is often the right kind of prayer."

"I don't really know how to do that—I mean, pray. When I think of prayer, it seems to me that people are always in the ask mode, and that would make me feel like I'm begging. The truth is,

I haven't been willing to ask because my life has been difficult, and asking would make me feel that I was demonstrating weakness and not being self-sufficient. You're probably suggesting that I should be asking God to help Tommy through this cancer."

"You can," McRae said, carefully, "but it needs to be in the context of God's will being done. You won't like this, Brian, but God doesn't march to your drumbeat. You need to get in step with Him."

We were quiet for the next minute or two, listening to our feet hit the ground, and I noticed that our rhythm had become a common one—we were running in unison.

"Let me try it this way," he said. "I believe that when you pray, you're trusting in God, not begging God. There's a difference. Because honestly, there will be a day when Tommy will take his last breath."

I stopped dead in the street, anger and tears welling up all at once.

"He's only eleven years old," I said. "What are you talking about?"

"I'm sorry," McRae said, meaning it. "What I'm trying to say is that all of us at some point take our last breath. Tommy's finitude, the end of life, is not something any of us can debate. It's a reality. None of us is infinite. We all will leave this earthly plane someday."

"But not now," I said through gritted teeth. "Not Tommy."

McRae left that declaration alone. He took another tack.

"Here's the point. What I believe is that when any of us, including Tommy, take that last breath, our lives are not over—because I believe in Jesus' resurrection. You're probably all ready to jump on me and ask why—but here's the bottom line, Brian. I've seen too many people take their last breath to ever doubt it. I've witnessed people stepping over from this life to more life and felt

God's presence welcoming them, not only from this side but to the next, so I just can't doubt in the resurrection. Now I admit I haven't been there myself, but at some point I have to trust what I've seen and what I've heard people say—most particularly Jesus."

"What did He say?" I asked, still edgy.

"It's simple," McRae said. "Jesus says, 'I am the resurrection and the life.' He says it every year to us at Easter. Let me tell you about a friend of mine. His name was Daniel, and like me he was a Presbyterian pastor. Daniel had prostate cancer, and despite all of the surgeries, the chemotherapy, and the radiation, after six years he knew his time was up. He used to tell me that cancer was a lousy dance partner because it was always stepping on your toes. Anyway, in the last six months when he couldn't do his job, he resigned, and I had to watch him waste away. I know this is hard for you to hear, but let me finish.

"Now, Daniel had, all through his ministry, stood by the bedsides of parishioners in exactly the same situation, so he knew what was coming. Oh, pick up those fourteens. Another speed bump. Still, he continued to always be the host when we visited him, even when we would gather around his bedside. He was still trying to host, even when he couldn't speak anymore. So then it became our privilege just to abide with him. I'm not talking about Tommy now. I just want you to have a perspective. It was our privilege to abide with someone we loved, with Daniel.

"You see, Brian, your presence is the best gift you can give Tommy, because he loves you, just as God's presence is the best he can give all of us because He loves us. So our goal became to help Daniel walk comfortably through the door and into God's embrace. It was near the end, and I had the two a.m. to six a.m. shift. There were a bunch of people sleeping on the floor, just because they wanted to be close.

"So I was sitting there in the dark thinking, *What will I do?* I picked up Daniel's Bible, turned to the book of Psalms, and started to read Psalm 1. It talks about how a righteous man is one like a tree planted by the river, who bears leaves and fruit and is full. I read the psalms out loud, and at the end of each one I'd stop and let all of those incredible images fill my head and my heart and the room. And at that moment, I did not have one doubt in either the presence or the love of God.

"Uneven road coming. Look, sometimes life provides us with moments that we just rest in, rather than being restless. That's why your wife and I so want you to find God. I kept reading the Psalms. Psalm 22 and 23 are about Jesus on the cross and forgiveness and then goodness and mercy following us through all the days of our lives. This is the philosophy of the shepherd, God as our shepherd. Some of the psalms were so sad they made me weep, but I actually read some that early morning that made me giggle out loud with joy. Anyway, I went all the way through.

"By then dawn was breaking over the horizon, and I decided I needed something more because I could feel death crowding the room. So I needed to read the resurrection story. I turned to John's Gospel, and I began with chapter 13, the upper room where Jesus washes the feet of the apostles and how awkward that was for Peter. And I remembered how easily Daniel had loved all of us because he was so secure in his faith. And then, most important, there was the conversation about the Holy Spirit and how we will always be comforted.

"So by the time I got to Jesus in the Garden of Gethsemane, people started to wake up, and they listened as I was reading about Jesus being betrayed by Peter and beaten by guards. We imagined him carrying the cross up to Golgotha and the sound of nails being hammered into his hands and feet, and then finally in death, his giving up and saying, 'It is finished.'

"You say these words out loud in a roomful of people, and you get the sense that there must be something present. I mean, for all of us, the death of Jesus was right there. We kept going and turned the page and began to read about resurrection morning, and we read about Jesus talking with Mary, along with Thomas and his doubts and Peter and John, and I swear we could almost hear him speaking with Daniel, not in specific words or terms but in presence. And it is in His Holy Spirit, His holy presence that God unites with us, becomes one with us.

"I want you to understand something, Brian. Nothing could deny the reality for me of Christ in that room during those most special moments with my friend."

Again, we were quiet, just running. This time I broke the silence. "As a lawyer, it seems to me that you perceive there is a preponderance of evidence that speaks to the loving presence of God. Is that right?"

"Let me put it this way. I'll just keep believing in a good God for you until you decide whether to come around."

"Now you sound arrogant," I said. "Your friend lived a full life, served his church, loved his family. But I've got a child with cancer who's only eleven years old. He hasn't even had a chance. He's just beginning. He's living in his dreams every night all the possibilities for his future—to pitch in the big leagues." I began to cry.

"You're trying to tell me that if we lose . . . if Tommy dies, I'm supposed to believe that God will immediately take him into heaven? We'll be alone, our son will be gone, and I'm supposed to believe that that's okay? Well, let me tell you something. It doesn't work for me, so where's your God now?"

This time Clayton laid a gentle hand on my arm and came to a stop.

"Brian," he said softly, "I know we're new friends, but I guess you need to understand where I'm coming from if you're going to believe anything I say. Like you, I had a wife, the light of my life. Her name was Adriana, and we had a beautiful little boy like your Tommy. God has both of them now. Six years ago, an automobile accident took their lives, and I believe with my whole heart and soul that they're in heaven, waiting for me."

I was taken back, unable to speak, and for a moment we just stood there, absorbing the importance of the link that was being forged between us.

"Brian, I think that living is a constant letting go. Don't get me wrong. I'm not suggesting any of this is easy or that God takes the pain away. But here's what I know: God will never betray you. He will never abdicate His love for you—or for Tommy. And if you can give Tommy to God today, tomorrow, the next day, He will—as the Irish say—hold your son in the hollow of His hand and embrace him in His bosom."

"But he's my Tommy. He's not God's Tommy. I love him. I'm the one who could lose him."

Clayton was loving but unwavering. "Actually," he said, "he is God's Tommy, and God loved him long before Tommy was even a thought in your mind. I promise you, Brian, God will love Tommy forever, no matter how all of this plays out.

"Hey, let's walk. We're almost back to the house, and I know this has been quite an ordeal. You know, running is supposed to be fun. I'm sorry. I know this hasn't been anything like that for you, but maybe it's been helpful."

"I'm not sure," I said. "But do you have time to run again someday, so I can ask more questions?"

"Oh, sure," he said. "That's what I'm here for."

"Okay, thanks." We stepped into my driveway, and I added, "Listen, maybe God brought you into our lives for an important reason. I mean, I'm starting to think there might be a critical reason you're here, so I mean it when I say thank you."

chapter 14

I don't know if it was denial or hope, optimism or avoidance, but in my mind Tommy seemed to be getting stronger every day. Oh sure, the therapy on his right arm was difficult, painful, and slow, but there was a goal in it—to gain the use of his limb—and in that effort, he became singular in his focus. His physical therapist told us that she had never worked with a child so intent. Tommy was competing, and that competitive spirit was a powerful force applied toward getting well.

I was back putting in normal hours at work and commuting by boat a couple of times a week with Rev. McRae rather than having Randy pick me up. We had shared a few more runs, and the minister had become a terrific guide. By the end of our third effort, I didn't have to hold his arm anymore; we just touched elbows, or I ran in space, confident that my new friend would tell me if there was any danger coming.

Our friendship was developing, as it always did when you shared the joy of sports with someone. I had not raised more questions of faith, I suppose because I was happy living in the eye of the hurricane with Bridgette, Tommy, and Shannon. We were in the storm, no doubt, but for the moment there were patches of sunlight. Call it Tommy's happiness parting the clouds of fear and doubt.

Bridgette was homeschooling Tommy, but he was beginning to renew communication with his classmates. He even had a couple of sleepovers with friends who didn't seem to notice his bald head or the limited use of his arm.

I was starting to think that children had a far better sense of acceptance than we did as adults. Maybe their picture of things was not confused by the ramifications of life. Not to say that they didn't grasp the significance of life's dramas and emotions, but it seemed to me that they were more linear in the way they processed the ebb and flow of changing information.

Bridgette was planning a Halloween party that would happen a week before Tommy was to go back into the hospital for the next round of chemo. It was to be a major event, with the house and the yard turned into the best ghoulish environment we could create.

Bridgette, Tommy, and Shannon were very excited for All Hallows' Eve, but I had no interest in what I consider to be a rather ridiculous celebration. As a kid I never liked to trick-or-treat, probably because costumes never meant much to a blind guy, but more, not being able to see took away the desire to be some other character. I laughed, remembering that somehow I must have felt that it was tough enough just to be Brian O'Connor, let alone making believe I was Zorro waving a sword around that could take someone's eye out.

Anyway, the family was excited—right up until once again we were swallowed up in the rotational violence of the hurricane.

Arriving home from work and entering the house around six-thirty in the evening, I was a little surprised because there was no immediate greeting from my family. I wasn't the only one. After I removed Bailey's harness and leash, the big dog made a circuit around the living room, dining room, and kitchen, finding no one. He charged upstairs, his nose active, and stopped outside Tommy's door as I gained the top of the landing.

For some reason my stomach tightened, and I took the last part of the stairs two at a time, arriving at Bailey's side. I knocked on my little boy's door.

"Come in," Bridgette said.

Entering the room, Bailey bounded to Tommy's bed, where Bridgette and Shannon were sitting. I learned Tommy was at his desk when I asked if there was something wrong.

"Tommy had some bad news," Bridgette said.

"What is it, pal?" I asked.

My son answered without turning his head. "Shaniqua died."

"Shaniqua died?"

"Tommy's been texting Shaniqua for a couple of days," Bridgette told me, "and he hasn't been getting any response. This afternoon I got a call from her mother. Her leukemia relapsed, and she died last night."

"I can't believe it," I said. "When Tommy and I met her, she seemed so happy. I remember she was playing—"

Tommy interrupted. "She was playing Mario Brothers," he said, his voice seeming to come from a great distance away. "When she played the game, she was always talking about being grabbed by the creatures or falling into the pit. She didn't play the game like other kids. I think she believed that the game was what was going to happen to her."

Bridgette said, "Shannon, come on downstairs and help me get everything ready for dinner. Let's let Dad talk to Tommy up here alone. Okay?"

"Okay," the little girl said reluctantly.

And the two of them left, leaving Tommy, Bailey, and me quiet for a long time.

I finally said awkwardly, "Do you want to talk about Shaniqua, pal?"

"She died," Tommy said woodenly, as if that pronouncement was all that mattered. "She died because of cancer."

I started speaking too fast. "Yes, but Tommy, there are many kinds of cancer. All different kinds. And they affect people differently. You know, like the cancer you have. The doctor said it's all gone. It's nowhere in your system. They've repaired your arm, and even though you're going to have more chemo, that's just to be sure it never comes back."

"Dad," Tommy said, not buying my argument, "Shaniqua and I have been talking. I know what a relapse is. And I know that the doctors told Shaniqua and her family that there was a good chance she was okay and that the leukemia was gone. Up until a couple of weeks ago, she thought she was all better. She was planning to come to our Halloween party. She said she was going to dress up as Beyoncé, and she was really excited." He took a deep breath. "We don't really know what's going to happen to me, Dad, do we?"

I was fighting back tears, humbled by my son's strength and wanting to find the words that would offer a hopeful perspective. I found myself saying something that made me sound like Rev. McRae, except that I knew I was only paying lip service to the idea.

"Tommy, there are things in life that just don't have answers or reasons for happening. Sometimes it's up to God to decide on the direction our lives take, and sometimes we just don't understand why He lets things happen the way they do. I've been talking to Rev. McRae about it, the chaplain at the hospital. He's a really bright person, and maybe it would do you some good to spend some time with him. But Tommy"—I put my arm around my son—"you're getting better. I know it. And I believe you're going to get rid of all of this cancer and pitch again, even if it's left-handed." I tried to smile.

Tommy was quiet.

"Dad, I don't know why God let Shaniqua die, but maybe she is up in heaven."

"I'm sure she is," I said. "Would you like to talk to the reverend about all this?"

I heard Tommy nod his head.

"Okay," I said. "I'll go downstairs and help your mother and Shannon with dinner. You stay up here as long as you want. And if you don't come down, I'll check with you in a while and see if you'd like your mother to bring you some dinner. Maybe you need some time by yourself to think."

Again, Tommy nodded.

"Call me if you need me," I said. "We can talk some more if you want to."

Tommy didn't come down for dinner that night, and he didn't want any food in his room when Bridgette went up to see him.

As we tucked Shannon in, she asked, not really as a question but more as a statement, "Tommy's not going to die, is he, Dad?"

"No, princess," I said. "Tommy is not going to die. The doctors believe there's no more cancer anywhere inside him. It's going to take a little while, but he's going to be well again, and everything will be just like it was before he got sick."

"But everybody dies sometime, don't they?" Shannon asked.

"Yes, we do," I said, "but most people live all the way until they're very, very old."

"Older than Gramma and Grampa?" Shannon asked.

"Much older than Gramma and Grampa," I said.

"Then why did Tommy's friend Shaniqua die?"

Once again, I played the God card.

"Because God wanted her in heaven with him," I said.

"What if God wants me in heaven?" Shannon asked.

"Well, I just won't let Him have my princess," I said, hugging her. "My princess is going to stay right here with her mommy and daddy. Okay?"

"Okay," Shannon said, hugging me in that special way reserved for fathers and daughters.

"You go to sleep now," I said.

And with the innocence of a child, she did.

I don't know if Tommy was asleep when I looked in on him. His breathing was slow and even. But when I said, "Tommy, are you asleep?" he didn't answer me, so I left him alone, closing his door quietly.

Moving back downstairs, I found Bridgette sitting in the living room, knitting. I could hear the sound of her needles as they moved. She never had been much of a crafts person, but I had noticed that over the years whenever she was under stress, she knitted or crocheted or did something else with her hands to relieve her tension and put her mind on something besides the problem.

"Everybody's asleep," I told her. "At least I think so. Tommy maybe just doesn't want to talk to anyone, but when I checked on him, his breathing made me think he was out for the night."

"What did you two talk about?" she asked.

I knelt down next to her chair and put my arm around her, almost losing it.

"Life, death, and cancer," I said. "Tommy really wanted to understand why Shaniqua died. I tried to convince him that his cancer was gone and that he would be okay, but he kept talking about how anything like this could ever happen, so we started to discuss God and His role in life and death."

"It's coming at you from all sides, isn't it, Brian?" Bridgette asked. "You're talking with Rev. McRae, and now Tommy is asking you questions you don't have answers for."

"Neither do you," I said a little sharply.

"No," she agreed. "But what I do have is faith, and like I told you before, maybe we're going to need it. Tommy's doing very well right now, but I believe this is the time to examine some of the important questions about our lives here on earth and the afterlife.

"Brian, I'm praying with my whole heart that Tommy will be okay, but I'm also praying that God will give us the strength to handle whatever fate may have in store."

"Fate?" I said. "What do you mean fate?"

"Fate," she said again. "Destiny."

"But Bridgette," I said, arguing, "there are all kinds of factors in this conversation. You know, genetics and cells, all the things that Dr. Hennessy has been talking to us about that are causes for cancer. It's all so complicated."

"Yes, it is," she said, "and that's exactly why it all has to be about the best medical treatment, faith, and yes, fate."

I got up from the floor and paced around the room, banging my shin on the coffee table.

"Why?" I exploded. "Why is this happening to our little boy? Why is this happening to us?"

Bridgette stood and hugged me.

"Brian, there is no answer to the why, but maybe there are some answers in how we cope with it. So keep talking to the reverend, and keep thinking about it."

"I told Tommy about Clayton," I said. "I asked him if he might like to speak to the minister."

"What did he say?" Bridgette asked.

"He nodded his head."

"All right," she said, "let's arrange for Tommy to have some time alone with Rev. McRae."

I was not really sure if Tommy ever gained the blessed peace of sleep that night. But that night was a turning point in the lives of our family. None of us would ever feel the same way about anything after Shaniqua's death.

chapter 15

I don't think I slept at all that night following my conversation with Tommy. It was one of those nights that everyone has, when your thoughts turn over and over in your head and seem to go faster and faster as the night wears on. Just as the night doesn't ever seem to end, your thoughts have no real conclusions. They hang in the air, suspended by strands of doubt and confusion.

I was scheduled to run the next morning with Clayton and as dawn broke I found myself becoming more and more upset over Shaniqua Adams's death and what it meant to Tommy O'Connor. Psychologists call it transference, and somehow that's what I was doing with Rev. McRae. He was the God symbol, so he was going to have to bear the full onslaught of my rage, disgust—and yes—hatred of any God who could ever take an innocent child.

For the first fifteen minutes of our run, that's all we did—just run. I suppose McRae sensed I was upset, because he finally said, "Well, we're feeling very friendly this morning, aren't we? Are we going to have a conversation, or is this run all about silence and contemplation? If it is, that's okay, except I hate to hear myself breathe this hard when we're running up a hill. It makes me think that I'm getting old."

"Did you know Shaniqua Adams?" I asked. "She's been in and out of the hospital with lymphocytic leukemia."

"A beautiful child," he said. "Yes, I knew Shaniqua."

"Well, then you know she died last night," I said, acid in my tone. "And your God let it happen. And you know what, Reverend? That sucks. Tommy and Shaniqua were becoming wonderful friends. They played video games together and were talking and texting all the time. And last night, Tommy talked about Shaniqua's death and the possibility of his dying. He's scared and angry and sad, all at the same time. So you've got to tell me, why do bad things happen to good people—most particularly, children? Doesn't the Bible tell us that they're God's innocents, and that He loves them? So why would He let them die?"

To his credit, McRae didn't hide behind some religious mumbo jumbo. "Honestly," he said, "I don't have a good response for you or Tommy. There just isn't an easy answer you can wrap your arms around, and frankly, when I'm confronted with a circumstance like this, it's my question too. I think it's this way, Brian. There just seem to be rules the universe runs on that are not understandable. I supposed they're what we call mysteries, unfathomable by the human mind. I'm hesitant to say it's not fair, but you can't help thinking that.

"Now on a good day I seem to be able to handle the doubt factor, but I know that on this morning you can't even consider that. Cancer is a horrible wild card. I could argue that it only arises out of our own physical makeup as human beings, our genetics, but I know you would come right back and say, 'Well, if we're all God's creations, then how can any loving God allow this to happen?'"

"A little while ago, you told me that I was supposed to be able to count on resurrection," I reminded him. "Well, you know what?

When I see the pain my son is going through during chemo—the sores, the fevers, and all the rest—I say who cares about resurrection? I'm living in this life, and I love this child who's suffering. You keep trying to tell me that this resurrection is out there. Is that the best you've got? Is that the best we get?"

"Okay," he said. "I can't say that's fair either. I know it doesn't provide you with any peace. I get that. You have every right to be angry."

"I'm more than angry," I said. "I want to deny God, to deny His existence."

"You can do that," McRae said, quietly. "You can deny the existence of God, but what good does that do Tommy? All along, Brian, you've been telling me—and I agree with you—that none of this is fair. That Tommy doesn't deserve to go through any of this. But on the other hand, do any of us deserve God's love? I mean, really? Have we truly earned it?"

"What are you talking about?" I nearly screamed. "This business of 'deserve or not deserve'? What do you mean?"

"Well," he said carefully, "what makes you so confident that you deserve to be resurrected? The only thing any of us can count on is the grace God offers us in Christ, the free gift He offers. It's His promise, you know. Jesus said, 'He who believeth in me gets the whole enchilada.' Now, disease or accident or war or pestilence—like the Bible says—these bad things happen to good people. So I suppose we have to think of them as tests of faith."

I exploded. "Look, McRae. Tommy doesn't need a test. Life and death and pain and suffering—a little boy doesn't need that. Tommy told me that when Shaniqua Adams played video games she played them as if they represented life and death, all of her fears. She played so afraid to lose, and now she's dead. And I don't know if she believed in your God or not, but what I do know is that in the conversation that she had with Tommy she was scared to death! Scared to die!"

"Listen, Brian. What God is offering, whether you believe it or not, is the gift of eternal life—life beyond this life!—not limited by the bonds of our physical death. And let me say again, I agree with you, no one deserves to suffer. What we're dealing with is the playing out of man's physical being on the earth. And in that context we are forced to cope with the vulnerability of our humanity. And Brian," he said, touching my shoulder, "that includes cancer. And neither child, neither Shaniqua nor Tommy, deserves to go through this. They do not. And that is something we clearly agree on. No child should ever have to suffer this way. I can't and won't try to offer you one logical reason that anything was right about any of this. In fact, Brian, everything says it's wrong. And I understand from the bottom of my heart that's how you feel."

"So all my life," I went on, "I've heard people talk about this thing called redemption. What's it all about? What is being redeemed?"

"All creation," he said. And I still didn't know what he meant. "All creation," he reiterated. "I don't believe anyone is left out of God's plan for creation. And all I can say is it ain't logical. What I know is that we're invited to hold on to two truths. One is what I've already said: there's nothing logical about cancer or any bad thing that happens to a good person. None of it is deserved. I want to be sure we're clear on that. But there is a caveat." And I could hear a smile come into his voice.

"What's that?" I asked.

"Well," he laughed, "the stupid crap we do to ourselves. I mean, the stuff we bring on ourselves."

"Yeah, okay," I said. "I get that."

"But Brian," he continued, "you have to understand the other truth."

"Which is?"

"We don't deserve all the grace we get either."

"Grace?" I said.

"Yeah, grace," he said earnestly. "I believe each of us is given by God the grace to cope with any of the circumstances life and our humanity presents us with, and I believe you are a classic example."

"Oh, sure. Here we go. You're going to tell me about the noble blind person. Right? The fact that I've been successful in life. I've overcome my blindness. You're going to tell me that that's because of grace—the grace of God? Well, let me tell you something, pal: it's about hard work. It's about trying harder than anyone else and going the extra mile. It has absolutely nothing to do with grace."

"Oh?" he said. "Well, how's your hard work going to help you if Tommy gets worse? How's anything you've done with your life, coping with your blindness, going to help you and Bridgette and little Shannon if Tommy—"

"Shut up!" I yelled. "Just shut up! I'm not even going to acknowledge that idea."

"Brian," McRae went on, insistent, "I believe that whatever happens to Tommy, if you have faith in God, if you will trust his life to Christ—if you will trust your own life to Christ—trust in His redemption, His resurrection, and in the power of prayer, you will be provided with the grace to cope."

After a while I asked, "So what is grace? You keep talking about God's grace, but what is it?"

"Undeserved love," he said quietly. "Grace is God's unmerited love for us. Look, we've all screwed up. We don't deserve anything good from God. That's why the Bible talks about redemption—

Jesus becoming the God-man as our Redeemer. Through Jesus, God promises us redemption. And His singular desire is to provide us with the grace necessary to complete our journey. We don't deserve God's grace, but it's His gift to us."

That was more than I could handle. "What in the world are you talking about? My little boy deserves all the grace your God's got. Maybe he's"—and I said it—"maybe he's dying. Who is this God anyway? You're saying my child doesn't deserve His grace?"

McRae's tone was gentle, patient. "Let me ask you something, Brian. Do you believe you deserve your parents' love?"

"I don't know," I said, thinking about my father.

"Well, try it this way. If love has to be deserved, is it really love? Think about Bailey, your guide dog. Do you believe he thinks he deserves your love? Or do you think you deserve to be loved the way you are by that beautiful animal? I don't really think that *deserve* and *love* belong in the same sentence. I think they're juxtaposed, not fairly connected."

"Okay," I said. "I grew up in the Catholic faith, and everything I was taught was sin, sin, sin and that I didn't deserve God's love. I kept hearing it in every prayer. 'I'm not worthy. I'm not worthy.'"

"I think you're being a little hard on the Catholic Church," he said. "But okay, for now, let's say you grew up thinking you weren't worthy of God's love. So when something wonderful happened to you, you were told that this was God's gift. The thing is, I believe we're operating in semantics. God's grace, or call it His hope for us to be resurrected and redeemed, is His constant. And I'll tell you something: it never varies. You've heard the phrase 'as constant as the North Star.' Well, that's God's grace. It's always there. It's never further away than our asking for it."

"But you don't always get what you want," I said. "Bridgette is praying as hard as any human being can that Tommy will be well, but we just don't know."

"Yes, but that doesn't mean that all of you will not be given the grace necessary to complete the journey. Love," he went on, "is God's gift. I know you believe, in human terms, that Bridgette, Shannon, and Tommy are gifts in your life. Well, God gave you those gifts. He provides gifts and grace and love to each of us, and we become more open when we create dialogue with God that allows Him to point the way.

Clayton thought while we ran for a while. "Look, we may have been going down the wrong path. The original question you asked was why bad things happen to good people. You asked what Tommy did to deserve this, and my answer is nothing. In fact, if anything, the idea of 'deserve' creates the dark side of our humanity because we then believe we are entitled, and in saying we're entitled we set up the blame game so we can blame each other and in the end blame God when things don't work out exactly the way we want.

"You know what it's like? It's as if we've become God's accountants, keeping track of debt and obligations, His and ours. That's not something a good relationship involves. The process of prayer and faith, of hope and grace, should be as free-flowing as the purest mountain stream, without being dammed up by our sense of entitlement. Listen, nothing in the gospel is about scorekeeping. We're not supposed to operate like that."

"So what tools do we have?" I asked. "What tools are we given that allow us to eliminate the idea of deserving love and replace it with accepting love?"

"Nothing but God's presence," McRae said simply. "His encompassing, complete, and total presence in our lives—in every aspect of the world as we know it, in the resurrection to come, and life everlasting.

"You know, I'm reminded of a theologian named Robert Capon. Capon said to imagine that it's snowing in Nebraska, and you're out in the middle of nowhere, and your car goes off the road, and you're stuck in a snowdrift. You're out there all alone, just you and your car. You're out of gas, and the motor has died, and it's fifteen below outside. Now, you know right there and then that you're going to die. And you ask where God is in all that. The answer, Capon says, is very clear. God is there, right there in the car, dying with you."

"Oh, forget it!" I blurted out. "Forget it. God?" I said, looking up. "That's not good enough. Get off Your ass and do something! Help my son! He doesn't . . . "

And now McRae yelled. "Don't you say 'deserve'!"

"But if He's a loving God," I said, yelling even louder, "He should help Tommy. Where is His love manifested? How can I see it?"

"Now, that's an interesting question," McRae said calmly. "How can you see God's love? Remember the hymn, 'I once was lost but now am found, / Was blind, but now I see'? You're asking the question, aren't you, Brian? 'How can I see it?' Consider that whenever Tommy is in pain, like the guy in Nebraska, consider that God is right there weeping with you and Tommy, crying with you, feeling for you.

"Brian, I know that when I take my last breath, I won't be alone because Jesus will be there. He'll be there ready to welcome me home, to fill me with the peace and the grace that I only get a glimpse of every now and then, to make me whole—body, soul, and spirit. And when you think about it, in the end, we all want that, don't we?"

I was beginning to feel exhausted. We slowed to a walk.

"I'm praying like crazy for your son's health and wholeness. I'm unashamedly badgering and pestering, beseeching and demanding God's help to maintain Tommy's life. I'm directly saying, 'Please heal this little boy.' I'm doing this without any hesitation, one, because Jesus told us to; and two"—he touched my shoulder—"I believe God cares, and I'm joining all of the saints in heaven telling God that this little boy is worthy of life in its fullest."

I paused. "Can I ask you something?"

"Sure."

"Well, Bridgette's been suggesting that Tommy needs to have his own counsel. Someone to help him with his questions."

"I agree," McRae said. "It is his life, you know."

"Have you ever done this before? I mean, with children?"

"It's what we do every day in palliative care," he told me. "It's the hardest thing we do, but it's also the most gratifying because in the innocence of children, faith in something larger than themselves comes easier to them."

"You mean faith in God," I said.

We were walking up my driveway now.

"Yeah, that's right," he said. "Faith in God. Even if that's difficult for you to come to terms with."

"Well, I know he's going to ask you the tough questions right off the bat. 'Why did Shaniqua die? Am I going to die too?' So what are you going to tell him?"

"Frankly," McRae said, showing some slight irritation, "that's between Tommy and me."

"And God," I said sarcastically.

"That's right," he said. "And God. And so before I see Tommy I'll be praying that the Holy Spirit gives me the grace, the strength, to say the things that will touch Tommy's heart, ease his pain, and provide him with peace."

"All right," I said. "Will you talk to Tommy in the next few days before he starts therapy?"

"Let's think about that. Maybe the conversations ought to begin when he's back in the hospital. Let me give that some thought.

"Look, Brian, I want to apologize for the way I just spoke to you about not wanting to share with you and Bridgette the talks that Tommy and I are going to have. I believe this is a private matter between Tommy and God, with me as only a conduit. But let me say this. As far as the question of why Shaniqua died and whether Tommy is going to die, let me start with the second point. Yes, he is going to die. All of us will die, including you and me. But I know what's more important to him right now is why Shaniqua died. Because cancer took her life. That's the answer he needs to hear because he needs to cope right now with the material concept of his disease.

"Children deserve truth, and that's what I intend to give Tommy. So, yes, we're all going to die, and cancer took Shaniqua's life. That's what I can offer Tommy: the truth. But I'll also talk to him about many of the things we're sharing, and I hope, as I do with you, that he can embrace some of the ideas.

"Then I think we have to wait and see what Tommy is thinking and feeling and not apply our adult agendas to the way his young mind is working."

"Look, Clayton, I'm just trying to make sure he has all the tools, I mean every possible medical option, every emotional support—and, yes anything he can gain from spirituality."

"From God," McRae said.

"Yes," I said. "From God."

"Look, I need to tell you something else in real humility. I'm not trying to speak for God. I'm only a guide for you and anyone who chooses to ask. And to do that for Tommy, I'll use stories about Jesus and how He touched lives and defeated death, stories of real people who searched for God—and found Him! I have some great ones to share with your son, and I think they can be effective in helping him along his own path."

I heard the sincerity in the man's voice and felt compelled to say, "You know what? You're a good person, Clayton. I'm glad you've come into our lives."

"Well," he said, "I'm the one who's truly blessed. Our conversations are forcing me to challenge my own faith, and thankfully so far it's holding up pretty well.

"Hey, by the way, I've been thinking about something. You've got all those friends downtown in the DA's office, and you know a lot of mucky-mucks in Boston politics. What about running the Boston marathon next year with me and doing something about this disease?"

"You mean raising money?" I asked.

"Yeah. That's exactly what I mean. Dinero, my boy, dollars. I bet a blind guy and a Presbyterian minister running together could hustle a pretty good chunk of change."

I felt enthusiasm for this idea welling up inside. *Doing something about the disease,* I thought. *That's a cool idea.*

And so that's exactly what I said. "That's a cool idea. Can you work out a training plan? I mean, I've never done a marathon before."

"I've run over twenty of them, and I've read just about everything there is on training techniques, so I'll make up a schedule. If we begin training now in the fall, we'll work it out through the winter and then pick it up again heavy when the snow's off the ground, hopefully by the beginning of March."

"Okay," I said, smiling. "I'll start hustling the masses for the money."

The morning had been incredibly difficult, but it had ended with a sense of hope and a new feeling. Was it—could it be?—yes, it was the Holy Spirit.

chapter 16

I hated bringing Tommy back to the hospital, but my emotions paled in comparison to what Tommy was feeling. He had just begun to be healthy, just begun to gain the use of his arm, just begun to spend time with friends—and now all of that was being brought to an abrupt end because of the insidious specter of cancer.

Bridgette was calling him for the fourth time. "Come on, Tommy," she said. "We have to go now. We need to be at the hospital to check in by ten."

There was no response coming from our son, and his bedroom door was closed.

"Brian," Bridgette said, "will you go up there and talk to him? He's not listening to me."

Arriving at Tommy's door, I found it was not only shut but locked. "Tommy," I called from outside his room, "let's go, pal. We have to go."

Still no response.

"Tommy," I said more urgently, "open the door. It's time to leave."

"I'm not going," I heard him say. "I feel good, and I'm not going."

"Tommy," I said, trying to be gentle, "you have to go to the hospital. I know you hate the chemo, but we have to do this together."

"You don't have to have the chemo. Mom doesn't have to be in pain. Shannon doesn't have to throw up. I do. It's my body. It's my cancer. And I'm not going."

His response surprised me and yanked at my heart. How to communicate at a moment like this? How could I express anything that would be meaningful to a little boy who had nailed the truth?

"Tommy," I said, "I want you to be strong and healthy, and chemo is the only way that can happen. You can't quit. Your mother and I and your sister need you to keep trying. We need you to be with us."

Then I heard Tommy crying softly from behind the door. "Please, Dad. Please don't make me go back," he begged.

And his weren't the only tears. I could barely control myself.

"Tommy," I said finally, "I'll be with you all the way, all the time. We'll handle this together. We need to work on this together. Please, open the door."

Finally Tommy allowed me in. I hugged him, and we stayed there holding each other for quite a while.

On the ride to the hospital, Tommy continued to alternate between stoic silence and quiet tears. Even Bridgette's maternal instinct could not offer real comfort to her son. We were all experiencing the same thing—a heaviness of spirit that we could not seem to shake.

I knew where Tommy was coming from. He had already been involved in more than fifteen weeks of chemo, and the idea of having to go back to what he knew was horrible made it even worse than when the therapy had begun. The old adage isn't always true, that knowing your enemy makes the battle easier. Sometimes knowing your enemy sets you up for depression when you have to face the problem again. Then, too, Shaniqua's death had brought dying directly into the equation. Now Tommy was being forced to confront all the possibilities of the disease.

About fifteen minutes into the trip, Tommy's attitude began to shift. The optimism and resilience of children began to find its way through the depression. He said things like, "I guess I need to keep eating to build up my strength, even when it's hard to get the food down and I'm not hungry."

"That's right," Bridgette said. "I know it's difficult, but that's the right approach."

"And I need to try to get as much sleep as I can," Tommy continued. "Rest makes you stronger."

"I agree," I told him. "Because your stomach will be upset, you need to sleep whenever you can and not worry about whether it's daytime or nighttime."

"And I need to hear stories about people who beat cancer," Tommy said, "so that I keep remembering to believe that I'm going to be okay."

"They call that motivation. We all need it. In fact," I told him, "Rev. McRae is going to be visiting you to talk about God. Is that okay?"

"Okay," Tommy said. "He seems like a good guy, and I have been saying my prayers, asking God to take away the cancer, so it's probably a good idea for me to talk with him."

"I like him, too," Bridgette said. "I think he's the kind of person who's good for all of us to know."

Arriving at Dana-Farber, I was very touched by the greeting Tommy got from the nurses and staff on the floor. On the one hand, I'm sure they hoped that kids didn't have to keep checking in and out of the hospital. All of the professionals who treated children wanted every child to be home, living a normal, healthy life. But on the other hand, whenever a child came back for more therapy, it meant that the child was alive and continuing to fight.

So Tommy's greeting was effusive, and I could feel the sincerity coming from everyone we met as we checked in.

The next day and a half was all about scans and tests, and we were extremely pleased when Dr. Hennessy informed us that things still looked good, both at the site and throughout Tommy's body. This should have been grounds for celebration. Fireworks should have gone off—but you don't do that when your child is taking drugs that cause sores in his mouth so severe that no medication can help him eat; when he spikes fevers that place him on the edge of delirium; when he doesn't sleep and you notice he's losing weight; and now the new thing—blistering on his hands and feet that made it virtually impossible even to put on a pair of slippers without pain.

And so, though the blue sky of cure was still out there, we couldn't see it very well as Tommy wrestled with the ever more intense side effects of the drugs that were meant to make him well.

* * *

And what about my little girl and life going on at home? We agreed that Bridgette would stay with Tommy at the hospital and Randy would become our driver for the day, as I took Shannon out for a special treat, trying to make up for the neglect that can happen when one sibling struggles for life and another lives it.

There we were in the American Girl store, and I was feeling like a bull in a china closet. Everything was feminine, frilly, and delicate, so I kept my hands close to my side to avoid knocking something off a shelf. Shannon was ecstatic as she searched for just that special doll—an American Girl that would become her friend.

I loved it as she babbled on. "Now, Daddy," she said, "after we find my new friend, we'll go to the restaurant and have an American Girl tea party, okay?"

"Okay," I said. "Tea it is. And what will we eat with our tea?"

"Crumpets," she said, "like in *Alice in Wonderland*."

"Do you think they have crumpets here?" I asked.

Shannon just laughed, and the sound was magical.

"Oh, I found her!" Shannon said, excited. "I found my American Girl, Dad."

"That's great, honey," I said. "Tell me about her."

"Well," she said, "she has short blond hair and beautiful green eyes."

"Why did you pick her?" I asked, not understanding. "Mommy says that usually little girls pick a doll that looks like them so that they can pretend she's their sister." For Shannon, that would mean a round, freckled Irish face with brown eyes and thick red hair.

"Daddy," Shannon said, her tone changing and becoming serious, "I want my doll to look like Tommy."

"Like Tommy?" I asked. "How come?"

"Because . . ." she said, leaving her answer hanging in the air.

"Because why?" I pressed, not getting it.

"Because if Tommy's not here . . . "

I reached out to touch her shoulder.

"Daddy," she said, her voice cracking a bit, "do you think they have any boy dolls? You know, so I can . . . " She was sobbing openly now. "So I can always have him with me?"

I swept my nine-year-old treasure into my arms, sure people were watching a father trying to console his daughter in a place where happiness was everywhere—except in the hearts of the man and little girl who were worried, very worried.

Tommy had been back in the hospital for two rounds of chemo and was trying to get his strength back to go on with round three. As before, I was amazed at the recuperative power of my son. During the five days leading up to the resumption of chemo, I happened to have the night shift when Clayton McRae ambled in, following a hospital dinner that wasn't very appetizing.

"Hey," he said, going right to Tommy and bypassing me, "the nurses tell me you're feeling a little better. Did your dad mention that I was going to come by and share some stories from what I think is the best book ever written—the Bible?"

"The Bible?" Tommy said. "I guess it has stories, but they all seem so Bibley."

McRae laughed. "Oh, man, some of the best stories. It's all about how you tell 'em. Wanna hear one?"

"Okay, but you don't have the book with you."

"Oh, that's all right," McRae said, chuckling. "I know these stories by heart, and I actually like to tell them with my own additions."

"Can I listen?" I asked, remembering that McRae had suggested in rather strong terms that his relationship with Tommy would be private.

"I guess so. You could probably use the story yourself." The reverend smiled.

"Okay," he began, "this is the story of David and Goliath. You may have heard it before, but I'm going to tell it a little differently. Now David was the youngest of all his brothers, and he was always thought of as the runt of the litter. I mean, he was really small, and he was the youngest son of a guy named Jesse. At the time, the people of a country named Israel were a mess because they couldn't figure out who their leader should be. Back then, they had guys who were called prophets. They were sort of like people with extrasensory powers. I mean, they could look into the future and tell you what was going to happen. Sort of like—what's that show on NBC?"

"*The Medium*," I put in.

"Right. *The Medium*. So prophets had these special powers, and the oldest and smartest of these guys was Samuel. He was the closest the people of Israel had to a leader, but it's funny—it gets a little complicated when religion tries to run a country."

I smiled. "I think you're going a little too deep."

"Yeah," he agreed. "Sorry. Anyway, the people were begging for a king, so, with God's approval they made this guy Saul the king. He was tall and handsome. He was kind of like a quarterback in the NFL. I mean, he had been a very successful warrior, and the people really thought he was cool. But the thing about Saul was that he loved himself more than he loved God."

I could feel McRae looking at me.

"Anyway, Saul turned away from believing in God because his ego got in the way, and he started to believe a lot more in himself than he did in God. The Bible says that God spoke to Samuel and told him that the Israelites needed a new leader. So Samuel, because he was inspired by God, went to Jesse's house and said he was looking for the next king. Ol' Jesse drags out his sons. He brought out the first three, but Samuel just didn't feel anything about them.

"Finally Samuel said, 'Hey, Jesse, don't you have another son?'

"'Well,' Jesse said, 'yeah. It's my little boy, David. He's out tending to the sheep. But you don't want to bother with him, because he's young and puny.'

"Samuel sighed and said, 'No. Bring him in. I want to meet him.' And as soon as he saw David, Samuel told everybody. 'This is the one. David is the one God has chosen.'

"So what's going on at the same time is that there were these guys called the Philistines, and they hated the people of Israel. They were causing all kinds of trouble. I mean, they were stealing cattle and ambushing people whenever they felt like it. In general, they were really messing with the Israelites. And then things changed because they found this big, bad dude named Goliath to be their leader. Let me put it to you this way: Goliath was so tall, he made Shaquille O'Neal look like a baby. He was as big as it gets, and he was one mean hombre.

"So Goliath decided that rather than lining up the armies and poking at each other with spears and swords, they should just go ahead and settle this. He said to Israel's army, 'You guys send out your best soldier, and if he beats me, we'll go back to our own country. But if he doesn't, I'm going to become everyone's king.'

"David's brothers were all in the army, and David kind of tagged along to be with his family. Everybody in Israel was scared of Goliath, but David wasn't. The story goes that young David went to a stream and found five smooth stones, and he put them in a bag. Nobody knew why—except David. He stepped forward and said, 'I can take care of his big guy Goliath.' People just looked at him and laughed.

"You know, Tommy, sometimes you can have an idea that seems crazy to everyone else, but if you believe in it enough you can talk people into letting you do what you want. So the soldiers figured that young David needed a whole bunch of armor, and they loaded him into all kinds of chain mail, so much of it that he couldn't even walk. He finally said, 'Listen, fellas, I'm going to take care of this dude the same way I protect my sheep against wolves and lions. I'm going to handle it with my trusty slingshot.'"

"A slingshot?" Tommy asked, incredulous.

"That's right!" McRae said. "Think about it. Here we have a young man believing that he could down a hulking Shaquille O'Neal."

"The giant," Tommy said.

"Yeah, the giant," McRae said. "What do you think made him believe that?"

"I don't know. I'd be scared."

"So would I," McRae went on. "But the Bible tells us that David believed he could defeat Goliath because he believed he had been selected by God. He believed that the Holy Spirit would give him the strength to slay the giant.

"So the next morning, David walked out in front of all the Israelites and all the Philistines without any armor, just carrying his slingshot and the stones. Goliath, standing up on a hill, laughed at him. He couldn't believe the Israelites had sent a boy to fight him. But David was really calm. Remember, he's full of the Holy Spirit. So he put a rock in the sling, and just like a pitcher he went into the windup, maybe even kicked his leg up, and then let the stone go. He hit the giant right in the middle of his forehead, and Goliath went down like a rock."

"David nailed him!" Tommy announced.

"You bet he did," McRae said. "The little guy took the giant down. You want to hear the rest of it, Tommy?"

"Yeah," Tommy said, and I could hear the enthusiasm in his voice. "What happened next?"

"Well, young David marched up the hill, and he picked up Goliath's sword. Then, just like hitting a home run out of Fenway Park, he swung the thing and chopped off Goliath's head."

"Yeah!" Tommy said.

I was smiling, thinking, *I think my friend just went a little too far.*

"Wow. I didn't think the Bible had stories like that."

"The Bible is all about human beings just like you and me and your dad who are trying to figure out how to put God in our lives," McRae said. "What do you think is important about this story, Tommy?"

"I guess the idea that David was little and the giant was big, but David could win?"

"I think you've kind of got it," McRae said. "God doesn't always choose big and powerful people to do important things. In this case, God chose David, the youngest of Jesse's kids, to do something great. You see, Tommy, in God's eyes size isn't an issue. There's an old phrase, 'It's not the size of the dog in the fight but the size of the fight in the dog,' and that's the way God operates. I also think that what's important in this story is that David was willing to hear God and believe Him. So he had the confidence—the courage—to kick Goliath's butt."

Tommy laughed, and I loved hearing the sound. "Yeah," he said. "David kicked the big guy's butt."

Now we all laughed.

"You know what I think, Tommy?" McRae said. "I think David understood that there was someone bigger than Goliath who would step in to help him. You see, David understood the simple truth that if he believed in God he could handle Goliath."

"Rev. McRae," Tommy asked quietly, "do you think my cancer is—well, is it sort of like Goliath?"

"I guess you could say that," McRae said. "The cancer is this big, scary thing, isn't it, Tommy? And the doctors and your parents are trying to figure out how to fight it. But maybe knowing that God's on your side will help."

I bit my lip, wanting to interrupt, feeling that McRae was presuming too much. But Tommy seemed to grab on to the idea, so I didn't have the nerve to say a word.

"So should I be asking God for help?" he asked McRae.

"You can if you want to," the chaplain answered. "But what's really important is for you to believe that God loves you and that He'll take care of you no matter what. We can pray for things, Tommy, but the most important thing is that we believe."

"Dad," Tommy asked, turning toward me, "do you believe in God?"

I don't know what my face said, but I tried to answer as honestly as I could, knowing the importance of the moment. "I'm working on it," I said, honestly. "Rev. McRae and I are working on it together."

"Mom believes in God, doesn't she, Dad?"

"Oh, yes," I said. "Your mother believes very much in God and prays to Him all the time." I felt compelled to add, "But Tommy, God doesn't do it alone. That's why we have all these wonderful doctors and this hospital working so hard to make you well."

Tommy asked, "If I really pray hard enough, why doesn't God just get rid of my cancer?"

"Your dad and I have been talking about this, Tommy. We don't know everything about God, but we do know that God always loves us. When it comes to your cancer, there's a lot we have to figure out ourselves. That's why you have the doctors and everyone helping you. I guess we have to put it all together—the things we do and then the things that God does. But for tonight, the most important part of our conversation is for you to think about something I am absolutely sure of, and that is that God loves you. He loves you a whole lot."

I heard Tommy sigh. "I'm a little tired," he said. "I think I'd like to go to sleep now."

"Okay," McRae said. "Thanks for letting me talk to you, Tommy. Can I come back again?"

"Oh, yeah. Your stories are cool. I want to hear more of them."

"That's great," McRae told him. "I'll come back real soon with another one."

Rising from his chair, I heard him pat Tommy's shoulder and then turn to me.

"We're running a long one on Saturday, right?"

"That's right," I said. My mind was full of the things Clayton had said. I wondered if I could accept, as Tommy had, the miracle God had performed in David's life as a sign of His love. Did God really have that kind of love for my son and me? If He did, what did it mean?

chapter 17

It was Christmas Eve, and thanks to Dr. Hennessy's good planning, Tommy's recuperative power, and the lack of the dreaded neutropenic fevers, we were home together as a family. Bridgette had gone all out for the occasion, decorating the house and playing Christmas carols nonstop for a week before the holiday.

Christmas hadn't meant much to me growing up because there was no real excitement, no Yuletide celebration in our family. Bridgette, on the other hand, loved Christmas—every bit of it. She could have been an elf, she was so full of Yuletide cheer, and this year she confessed to me that she was going a little overboard.

She kept saying, "We need some happiness around here. We need Christmas spirit. We need to love each other and not be burdened by Tommy's illness, even if it's only for a little while."

Easier said than done, I thought, but she was so ebullient that she pulled it off.

I actually found myself excited on Christmas Eve, especially because Shannon still believed in Santa Claus. She was a little bit past sitting on Santa's lap at the mall, but she still wanted to believe that a jolly old fat man and eight reindeer, and maybe Rudolph as the ninth, still brought toys and gifts to good little boys and girls.

She had written her letter at Thanksgiving. What she wanted most of all was a dollhouse that I found out came in a kit with one of those sets of directions only an engineer could read. I was worried. It didn't seem right for Santa to bring a boxed item. The joy for Shannon under the tree would be the dollhouse all put together.

So how was a blind dad going to handle that? *With the help of his intrepid son, Tommy,* I thought, who from a very early age had been one of those kids who could figure out how things went together. But we had a problem: Tommy did not yet have effective use of his right arm, though it was improving every day, and I was—well, I was blind, wasn't I? We discussed my problem in the garage, man-to-man.

"Okay, Dad," he said. "I've got an idea. Shannon and I will go up to bed early like we're supposed to, and after you know she's asleep come get me. Then we'll put this thing together. I can read the directions and find the pieces if you can do the fine work, putting bolts and nuts together."

"You really think we can do it?" I asked.

"Piece of cake, Dad," he said. "This isn't anywhere near as complicated as the Lego stuff I make."

"All right," I said. "Let's do it."

And so there we were, around ten o'clock on Christmas Eve, with the pieces of the dollhouse laid out all over the living room floor. Tommy had divided the parts into sections, and we had completed the basic framing.

Bridgette was furnishing me with eggnog, and Tommy actually had a little himself without the alcohol. We were a very happy father and son, working away together while Christmas carols played softly in the background, with Bridgette busy in the kitchen, making the stuffing for tomorrow's turkey.

Every once in a while she would go upstairs to make sure Shannon was asleep, and it seemed that she was.

I've heard it said that blind people are supposed to be able to hear better than other people, but the truth is that's not really the case. We just use our hearing with more proficiency. But on this night, I was so involved in my mechanic's role that I didn't hear my little girl come down the stairs and stand in the door of the living room, watching her brother and me putting together her Santa gift—the dollhouse.

I nearly jumped out of my skin when I heard her ask, "Dad, what are you doing?"

Getting up as quickly as I could from the ground where I was surrounded by future parts of the dollhouse, I worked my way over to where our little girl was standing as she asked again, "What are you doing? You and Tommy?"

I didn't have an answer, but thank goodness Tommy did.

"Shannon," he said, "go back upstairs and go to sleep."

"But that's my dollhouse," she said. "That's my special present." Now she was sniffling. "And Santa was going to bring that to me. Why is it here in pieces?"

Tommy hung in there. "I had this happen to me, Shannon. Remember a couple of years ago when I wanted that Schwinn racing bike?"

"Yes," she said.

"Well, I came downstairs just like you did, and I found Dad and Grampa putting it together. You see, sometimes Santa has to put big stuff in his sleigh in a box. There just isn't enough room for everything he has to carry. Dad and I were down here putting this together because we still wanted to surprise you with it under the tree."

"You're telling me a fib, Tommy," Shannon said, still crying. "There is no Santa Claus."

"Oh, yes, there is, Shannon," Tommy said, with real fervor in his voice. "There is a Santa Claus, and he loves all of us—all the children."

Tommy went over and surprised both Bridgette and me by putting his arms around his sister.

"I promise you, Shannon," he said, "there is a Santa Claus. You have to believe."

"Oh, okay," she said with hesitation. "If you say so, Tommy, I'll believe."

Bridgette joined them at the door.

"Come on, Shannon," she said, "let's go back to bed, okay? And let the boys finish their work down here. Why don't I read you the story of 'The Night Before Christmas,' and you can think about where Santa is, somewhere in the world, bringing toys to little girls and boys who are just as excited as you are."

They went upstairs, and I sat unable to continue working, so proud of my son.

"That was incredible, Tommy," I said, "what you just did for your sister."

"We all have to believe," he replied simply. "There are just things we have to believe in. I've been talking to Rev. McRae about believing in God, and he's explained more to me about how God loves us. God is in the beautiful things we see around us, like trees and the ocean and clouds. And God is inside all of us, in our hearts, if we just believe. Rev. McRae says that God will always love us and take care of us."

"So, you think Santa Claus is like God?"

"Oh, no, Dad," Tommy said quickly. "Santa Claus is make-believe, but God is real."

I didn't know what to say to my remarkable boy. Somehow, out of his cancer, he was forging a relationship with God far beyond anything I had been willing to experience. What I understood in that moment was that Tommy, my young son, was far more evolved as a person than his blind lawyer father. He was seeing things I was missing or wasn't willing to see, and I knew on that Christmas Eve that I would have to give the idea of God a lot of thought.

By Christmas morning Shannon had gotten over her Santa disappointment and was very pleased with the dolls her mother had picked out, who would be living in the house that Tommy and I completed around midnight.

Tommy was also delighted with the video games he received, along with a Wii that his grandfather was hooking up to the television, while the smell of turkey roasting made all of us hungry.

I had invited Clayton to join us, and he turned out to be a terrific guest, demonstrating a great sense of humor and interacting easily with all of us by bringing his guitar and playing carols that sang before dinner.

By the way, anybody who thinks that blind people are all musical should have been in the O'Connor house that afternoon. I am, for all purposes, tone-deaf. Stevie Wonder has nothing to worry about when it comes to my musical talent, but the day was fantastic and I sang out loud and off-key with a spirit I hadn't felt in months.

After Bridgette's fantastic dinner, the family got involved in playing the Wii game, selecting bowling as a team event. Tommy beat us all left-handed, and he was delighted.

"Maybe you have a future as a southpaw, bud," I said, and I could sense his smile.

Our guests had gone home at the end of a fantastic Christmas Day, and the O'Connor family lounged in the living room in that coma that sets in after you've eaten too much turkey.

It had been a tough day for Bailey because the smells of all the food had driven him crazy with the desire to taste everything. Because he was a guide dog, I had worked hard never to feed him scraps from the table, though sometimes I would put special treats on his food just to give him a change in diet.

Anyway, on this Christmas night I let Bridgette feed him some turkey that he had gobbled up in one bite.

Back in the living room he did not lie down in his usual place behind my rocking chair. Instead, he worked to squeeze up on the couch between Shannon and Tommy, and I decided to allow him his special Christmas privilege.

I heard the sound of Bailey snuffling and then Tommy's complaint.

"Bailey, cut it out! You're always doing that."

The dog was persistent, and I lost it.

"Bailey!" I said harshly, "cut it out. Stop smelling Tommy."

I heard the dog's collar jingle as he looked up at me and then went back to his sniffing.

"Cut it out, Bailey!" Tommy said again. "Leave my arm alone."

I jumped up from my rocking chair and tripped over the coffee table but got my arms around the big dog. For the first and only time in our relationship, I smacked the big animal hard on the shoulder.

"Down!" I said. "Down, Bailey."

The dog whimpered, clearly not understanding his master's behavior.

He jumped off the couch but stood there, unable to grasp what was going on.

I continued. "No! Bad dog! Get outside."

The dog ran through the kitchen, and I was right behind him. Breathing hard, I got to the back door, but before I could open it I'd realized what I had done.

"Come on, boy," I said quietly. "Let's go outside."

The change in my tone made the animal lick my hand. We stepped out into the cold Christmas night darkness. I had shoes on but no coat, and I dropped to one knee in the snow at the bottom of our back steps to put my arms around the animal's neck.

"I'm sorry, Bailey," I said.

The dog whined and licked my face.

"You have to be wrong, Bailey. You just have to be wrong."

Taking deep breaths of the frigid air I worked to gain control of my emotions before we stepped back into the kitchen.

Bridgette met us at the door. "You all right?" she asked.

"Let's talk about it after we get the kids to bed, okay?"

"Sure," she said, touching my cheek with the tips of her fingers.

We returned to the living room and tried to get things back to normal.

"Boy, Dad, you really yelled at Bailey," Tommy said.

"I know. It's just that I don't want him doing that smelling stuff. If he starts that habit around strangers, it could be embarrassing. Are you guys ready for bed? I think it's about time. It's been a wonderful Christmas."

"It's been a supercalifragilisticexpialidocious Christmas," Shannon said, remembering *Mary Poppins*.

"It's been the best Christmas I ever had," Tommy agreed.

"All right," I said, "let's call it a night."

After tucking the children in, Bridgette and I returned downstairs, sitting quietly together, neither of us ready to speak.

Bridgette finally broke the silence. "You think that Bailey smells something in Tommy's arm?" she asked, not really wanted me to answer.

"It happened before," I said, resigned. "I don't know, Bridgette. But we're not going to spoil this time for Tommy. Right now he's feeling well. Between now and the time we go back to the hospital for the next round of tests, we're just going to enjoy every moment we have as a family."

"You know," she said, "I was sitting here thinking about everything I believe in—God and His faithfulness, our family, our love—and in all of those things the central theme, the thing I'm sure of, is that love can overcome anything. That's what I'm going to continue to think, Brian. I'm going to continue to commit to the idea that our love and God's love and the love we feel for our children is enough to overcome this cancer, and for tonight, for now, I'm going to believe that Bailey is wrong."

"Okay," I said. "I agree with you." I put my arm around my wife. "Merry Christmas, Bridgette. I mean it. Merry Christmas."

chapter 18

"Ring out the old, ring in the new," they say to signal the beginning of a new year, full of promise and hope, full of resolution and reform. But in the O'Connor house on New Year's Eve, Bridgette and I were feeling only fear, apprehension, and, yes, even panic.

We alternated between dreading what Bailey had hinted at and being sure that the dog was just doing his doggy thing and that we didn't have to pay any attention to the animal's persistent behavior during the past week.

On New Year's Day, Tommy and I watched all the bowl games, with particular interest in the Orange Bowl because Boston College was playing Miami, and we both rooted with great enthusiasm for the home team. They won and Tommy was delighted.

The next morning, we made the drive that had become habit and checked Tommy back into Dana-Farber, where the scans that made us hold our breath began later that day. If Tommy was worried that his cancer would return, it didn't show in his behavior.

Ah, the resilience of optimism and youth, I thought.

To her credit, Dr. Jennifer Hennessy got right to the point concerning the test results. I suppose she had come to understand that being direct was always her best option in cases of life and death.

"Our tests indicate that there's renewed activity at the original site," she said, "and because of what we're seeing, I'm going to order some additional images."

"It's back? And you suspect some spread?" Bridgette asked. I felt her grip my arm.

"Let's not get ahead of ourselves," Dr. Hennessy said. "We just need to know for sure what's going on with Tommy. At this point I don't recommend that you say anything to him because we don't really know anything beyond the fact that there's some tumor activity at the primary site. If there's no metastasis, then we're still dealing with a localized circumstance that I believe we can control.

"I'm going to order a PET scan, because usually if this kind of cancer is developing, it happens in the shoulder area or in the lungs. Has Tommy indicated any unusual pain in his arm?"

"No, he hasn't," I said. "In fact, he's getting pretty good mobility. I've been amazed at the progress he's making."

I heard Dr. Hennessy smile. "He's a fighter, your Tommy, and I also think he's an optimist. Though I can't prove it scientifically, I've been fascinated with how much better kids with a positive outlook seem to do than those who allow the disease to get them down.

"I've already arranged to have the test done in a couple of hours, and with a little luck we'll examine the imaging before the end of the day. I'm sorry to put you through all of this. For as long as I've been treating children, I've hated having to place this kind of burden on parents."

"We want you to know," Bridgette said, meaning it, "that the O'Connor family thinks you're a pretty wonderful doctor. We know how hard you're trying to take care of our son."

"Thank you," Dr. Hennessy said, "but frankly, it doesn't make it any easier for any of us, most particularly Tommy."

The next few hours seemed like an eternity. There was no way for us to busy ourselves by reading a book or taking a walk or sharing in conversation. We just sat quietly and waited. There had been so much of that since the drama of our lives had begun. How many times had we been with Tommy while test after test had been run? How often had we waited for results, our lives suspended? And now, here we were again, waiting.

After what seemed forever, we were again in the conference room with Dr. Hennessy, and I knew immediately that this conversation was going to be one of the worst of my life.

I heard her sigh, take a breath, and sigh again. "Okay," she said finally. "Tommy has activity at the original site, and there is mets in his lungs."

"Mets?" I queried, my voice shaking.

"Metastasis," she said. "I've already discussed the surgical alternative to chemo, but frankly, there are too many tumors to approach the problem surgically."

Bridgette shattered, sobbing uncontrollably. I put my arms around her and held her while Dr. Hennessy waited.

"No! No!" my wife kept saying into my shoulder. "Do you understand what this means, Brian? The chemo didn't work. The cancer has spread. It's killing Tommy."

Dr. Hennessy intervened quietly. "We're not beat yet, Mrs. O'Connor—Bridgette—not by a long shot. Remember, we have other drugs that can fool these cells, and I'd like to change up Tommy's protocol and take another tack."

"Have you had success when you adjust the chemo?" I asked.

"Oh, yes," she said. "That's what this effort is all about. I mean, there are a number of drugs and drug combinations."

Bridgette asked the tough question. "If Tommy is dealing with metastasis in the lungs, has his chance for cure diminished considerably?"

Dr. Hennessy paused, and then her answer rang clear as a set of chimes. "Yes," she said quietly. "I won't lie to you. Tommy is a very sick boy. But I have been involved in cases where the chemo has been changed and the patients have done very well. It is true that his chance for cure has been reduced, but I don't believe it's time to look at this as an unmanageable circumstance. There is still a great deal that we can do, and I know it's important for all of us to stay as positive as Tommy. The feeling we give him will have a lot to do with the way in which he chooses to compete against the disease."

"Thank you, Doctor," I said. "We understand."

We understand. But did we? Could we? Could anyone get their arms around the feelings of despondency and loss that choke off hope when a physician tells you that your child's cancer has metastasized and that the possibility for cure has sunk lower?

In those brief seconds, I alternated between a depression that nearly took all of my strength and an anger that sent adrenaline pumping through my body. Reality was more than I could accept, and yet somewhere in the confusion I knew I had to stay present in that moment.

Dr. Hennessy continued, "Okay, we'll start Tommy on the new meds tomorrow," she said. "I know it's a lot to suggest that you try and make tonight as pleasant for him as you can, but I mean it when I tell you that every minute he feels good is a minute he's building more strength, and he's going to need that strength to fight this thing."

That was an understatement, I thought, but I found myself also thinking that somehow I believed Tommy had more ability to cope with the burden of cancer than either his mother or his father.

Have you ever had those moments in life when you laugh too much or try too hard to create an environment that you think makes everybody happy around you but actually makes all of them uncomfortable because you're being so weird? In retrospect, I'm sure that's how Tommy and Bridgette saw my behavior that evening.

As we watched movies, ate McDonald's, and played video games, I kept trying to fake cheerfulness. In fact, twice when I made some kind of bad joke, Tommy's response was, "Oh, Dad," meaning, *That was stupid.*

Because Tommy wasn't to begin the next round of therapy until the morning, Bridgette and I waited until Tommy fell asleep and then drove home around 10 o'clock to be with Shannon when she got up for school. This kind of parenting was the toughest part of our lives because I knew we weren't doing any of it very well. Though we both tried to be at home when Shannon woke up or went to sleep, we understood that our inconsistency must be extremely difficult for the little girl to understand.

When the chemo drip is initially administered, it takes a few hours for the nausea and other early symptoms to take effect. One of the worst parts of it for anyone is knowing what's going to happen. Though the doctors give you antinausea medications, they can't really eliminate what's coming. The medication can only modify the side effects.

And so, there we were with the poisonous, life-giving drugs flowing into Tommy's system and Tommy perceptively asking a question I so wished we could have avoided.

"Dad," he said, "why are there three bags of stuff instead of just one? Why is this different?"

I took a breath. "Well, Tommy, this time it's a different kind of chemo." And I used the phrase Dr. Hennessy had employed when she spoke to us about the new developments. "You see, Tommy, there's some activity at the primary site."

"You mean the cancer is back?" my little boy challenged, almost as if he expected it. He sounded strangely calm.

"Well, I guess you could say that," I told him, "but really, Tommy, it's just that—"

He interrupted, "It's just that the cancer is back, Dad, and they're giving me new stuff to try to kill it. Isn't that right?"

Bridgette took over. "Tommy," she said, "the doctors are using different drugs because that's how they outsmart the cancer. They keep changing up the medications so that the cancer cells can't get used to what's attacking them."

"But Mom," Tommy said, not missing anything, "the scans I've had over the last few months have been clear. Now you're telling me that there's more cancer, so the first stuff didn't work, right?"

"Well, I don't know if that's true," Bridgette said. "It's just that we didn't get rid of all the cells, so—"

"So I'm taking a new drug."

"Yes," Bridgette said, resigned. "You're taking a new drug."

I listened to this conversation as if it were coming from another world. Here I was, a lawyer trained in argument and rebuttal, and I had nothing to say because Tommy had the whole thing figured out.

The question now was whether to tell him about the metastasis, the spread of the disease into his lungs. Dr. Hennessy had indicated that she didn't believe that was necessary at this time, but I wondered if it would be better for our child to know all the facts so that he could prepare completely for the fight of his life.

Bridgette must have been thinking the same thing because she surprised me.

"Tommy," she said, "when I was a nurse I worked with a lot of patients who had cancer. Like I told you, it's hard to get rid of all the cells, and if they're in your bloodstream they move around. So that's why you take chemo for so long. Remember what Dr. Hennessy said? You'll have to go through this kind of treatment for quite a while to make sure that all the bad cells are out of your system, and we may hear that the tests show cells are showing up in different parts of your body. That's just the way this disease works. But you're doing very well, Tommy, and I know with Dr. Hennessy's help and our prayers everything will work out. That's what you told Shannon at Christmas, remember? You said you have to believe, right?"

Tommy must have nodded because Bridgette went on.

"We all believe you're going to be fine. We just have to cope with this chemo. Okay?"

Tommy's answer was to scrunch up his face and begin to retch, requiring his mother to hold a vomit pan to catch the projectile that emptied his stomach of whatever was still in it.

* * *

And so the cycle began again of chemo and sores and fever and depression and hope and fears, all competing in our hearts and minds. As I became aware of how often Bridgette prayed, I realized that on my next run with Rev. McRae, I desperately needed to learn how to ask God for His help.

chapter 19

I was scheduled for an early morning run with Clayton, but when he arrived he could tell I hadn't been sleeping at all.

"You look awful," he said.

"Great. Thanks for the compliment."

"No, I mean it. Something wrong?"

"Is it that obvious?" I asked.

"When you know what to look for," he said. "All that puffiness around your eyes suggests you've been crying, and your usual smile certainly isn't in place, so what's going on?"

"Look, would you mind if we didn't run this morning? I really need to talk to you, and I don't want to be distracted trying to pound our way up hills. Anyway, it's still only about thirty degrees, so how about a hot cup of coffee and some conversation?"

"That'll be fine," he said, seeming to understand. "Where's Bridgette?"

"At the hospital with Tommy. It was her turn last night. Let me take a minute to say good-bye to Shannon before she goes to school. The coffee's in the kitchen. I'll be right back."

After sending Shannon out to the bus, I returned to the living room with a second cup of coffee of my own and one for Clayton.

He sat down while I stood by the fireplace sipping on Starbucks Italian Roast.

"I take it Tommy's not doing so well."

"The cancer's back in his arm," I said, woodenly, "and there's metastasis in his lungs. They're going to try a new form of chemo. They tell us they keep changing the medicine in order to fool the cells, but you know, I'm wondering if they even have a clue about this disease. It just feels like a crapshoot when they give patients drug after drug and keep quoting statistics."

Clayton's voice was gentle. "I've been at this job for four years, and I have seen some tremendous breakthroughs. But I understand what you're feeling. Sometimes I get pretty down about the whole thing, too, especially when you see the kids suffer."

"Yeah," I said, sighing, taking another sip of my coffee. "Dr. Hennessy told me that the stuff Tommy is going to be taking during this round of chemo is even more reactive than before, and that was bad enough. So, you see, my spiritual friend, that's why I'm asking you for help."

"Of course," he said. "That's what I'm here for. What do you need?"

"Well," I went on, "I think I need to pray. Bridgette's been doing a lot of that, but I've come to the conclusion that it's time for me to get on the bandwagon." I smiled. "Maybe God has a special way of listening to fathers of sick kids who also happen to be blind. Maybe we get a special hearing because of our handicap. What do you think?"

"God hears everyone's prayers," Clayton said. "No one's left out. And you may not realize it, but when you pray, you're actually expressing, at some level, that you believe God cares enough to hear you and consider your request. And there isn't only one way to pray, because God knows what's in our hearts. But we can talk about prayer. Have you ever prayed before?"

"Oh, I said the words," I told him. "Remember, I grew up Catholic, so we always had to go to confession and do penance for our sins. So I said all the words, and I learned all the basic prayers like the Our Father and the Hail Mary, and then in confession the Act of Contrition, and then there was the rosary with all of its mysteries. And during Mass we recited a lot of prayers and the Apostles' Creed, stuff like that. But I never thought about what the words meant or how it all connected to God. So I need you to help me learn to pray. And, frankly, Clayton, I'm pretty desperate."

"Well," my friend said, taking a deep breath, "first, and most important, it's critical that you believe in God's commitment to meet us and lead us to life. That His love is reliable and true. That's what Jesus taught us, that's what we can learn from Him—to simply talk with God and then to listen to Him speak back."

"Okay," I said, "when you say God speaks to us, are you talking about in tongues or what? I mean, have you really ever heard God's voice?"

"Not actually," he said, and I heard him smile. "But I have clearly felt the prompting of—well, how can I express this?" He got up from where he was sitting and began to pace the room, stopping in front of me. "I've sensed . . . a divine nudge when my heart has felt the true presence of God.

"Brian, I know God hears us. The real question is, do we hear God? And if He doesn't speak to us audibly, how can we know His guidance, His help, His love? You see, I think prayer is a conversation, not a monologue. It is a true and honest conversation between you and God. It's the continuing of an ongoing relationship. We see it in the Bible, you know? There are all kinds of conversations. We tend to believe that God only responds to us in the big moments when in fact God's presence and communication are ongoing, consistent, committed.

"Look, here's an example. In the tenth chapter of John's Gospel, Jesus holds up the image of the shepherd, and He reminds us—all of us—that the sheep always recognize the voice of the shepherd. They know his voice. Jesus goes on to say that the sheep listen to the shepherd's voice. He calls his sheep by name. He leads them out. He goes ahead of them. The sheep are willing to follow him because they know his voice. Then Jesus says that He is our shepherd, and He speaks to His followers. He expects us to listen, to hear His voice and follow His direction, because that's what we as disciples of Christ do.

"Now I don't want to make light of this, but do you remember Lily Tomlin, the comedienne?"

"Sure. I used to love Ernestine," I said.

"Well, she asked, 'Why it is that when we talk to God it's called prayer, but when God talks to us it's called schizophrenia?'"

I laughed.

"Brian, my friend," he said seriously, "simply put, talking and listening to God are acts of faith."

I shrugged. "Look, Clayton, I know that I'm new at this and that faith hasn't been a big part of my life, but isn't it fair for me to think that God will hear me and understand the need that I'm trying to express in my prayer?"

"Absolutely," he replied, earnestly. "God always listens. But as I told you before, the real question is, are you open to hearing God's response?"

"Okay, but how do I learn to listen to God?" I asked. "How do I—what's that thing in the Bible—open my ears, open my heart, all that stuff?"

"You know, it wasn't easy for Jesus' followers," Clayton said, "even the people closest to him. Peter, James, and John had front-row seats to the greatest prayer guy who ever prayed, and they didn't always get it. You see, when Jesus prayed for something, it happened, and they wondered if that would be the case in their own lives.

"Obviously they wanted to be able to talk to God the way Jesus did. So one day one of them asked, 'Lord, teach us to pray.' Now, these guys had prayed before, kind of like you mentioned in the Catholic Church. They were Jews. They understood what prayer was. I mean, they were always offering prayers—before meals, at Sabbath, at the High Holidays. They weren't asking for the words. They were looking for something deeper.

"I do believe there is a sort of method to prayer. I think—and now I suppose I sound like a clinical psychologist—the interaction with God is a learned behavior. You have to practice talking and you have to practice listening. And you know what, Brian? I think you'll be great at it."

"You mean because I'm blind?" I said, a little sarcastically.

"Yes, exactly," Clayton said, not rising to the bait. "You have a unique ability to hear, don't you? I mean, you tell me all the time that you use your sense more broadly than sighted people do. Well okay, then plug into prayer and listen to God.

"Brian, I believe that in prayer, we ask three things. The first request: 'Forgive me my sins'—something we find in the Lord's Prayer. We need confession. It humbles us and reminds us that we follow a holy God but we fail, and we need forgiveness."

I interrupted, "But Tommy is just a child! What sins has he committed?"

"Ah, but in this conversation he's not the one offering up prayers, Brian. You are."

I wasn't sure how I felt about this part of my friend's conversation, so for the moment I decided to let it go.

"The second question is also like what we read in the Lord's Prayer, 'Give us this day our daily bread.' We ask God for what we need today—strength, hope, help. I'm convinced God wants us to ask with direct intention."

"Okay," I said. "I won't have any trouble with that part."

"You know, Brian, Jesus tells us to knock on the door. Name your need. Be persistent. We're supposed to ask, because we're God's children and He wants to give us what we need. This is how we build up trust, by asking God for what we need and watching Him respond.

"I've mentioned that God may not respond in exactly the way we intend. But that's where faith comes in—faith that in His enormous, unfailing love, He will respond in the best way possible, even if we don't completely understand it.

"Finally we ask, 'What do You want me to do?' In the Garden of Gethsemane Jesus prayed, 'Lord, not My will but Yours,' and this is our stance when we ask God what part we can play in the events going on around us. We ask for His guidance to do what He wants. We acknowledge His supreme knowledge and believe in His love. This is when the Holy Spirit enters our lives, because we've asked God for direction and help.

"In this part of the prayer we're clearly asking God to bless us and protect us. The Bible says Jesus understands our longings, because He came to earth as a man. He felt our pain, our suffering, our confusion. He even understands our temptations."

I nodded. I was keeping up okay, though I was hearing a lot of new information.

Clayton continued. "Clergy often talk about the idea of 'let go, let God.' This is the trust factor, and I bet that's going to be the hardest part for you. I think being blind you've never really let go or really trusted."

"Sure I have," I said, a little annoyed. "I've trusted Bridgette with my life, and every day I trust Bailey to do his job." The big animal, who had curled up at my feet, lifted his head at the sound of his name, and I scratched his ears.

"Okay. Well, maybe you do trust," McRae said, "so I guess you do sometimes let go and let God. It's my prayer that you'll make a conscious decision, as you begin to pray, to surrender to God, to allow Him to show you the way, and in that moment of true surrender you'll be open to hearing His response.

"There's a theologian named Walter Wink who said something really cool. He said that history belongs to the intercessors, those human beings who are willing to ask. You know, God gives us so much, but there is so much more He's willing to give if we would just ask.

"Here's how I want you to think, Brian. *You pray the future into being.* That's exactly what we're going to do about Tommy. We're going to pray as hard as possible to bring the future we long for into being."

I couldn't help it. I started to cry because in the depth of my heart that's all I wanted. And if praying the future into being guaranteed that Tommy would be okay, I knew that I would be on my knees for the rest of my life.

"All right," I said, sighing. "This is a lot for me to take in this morning. I promise I'll think about it, but could you help me with the first prayer—for Tommy, I mean? Could you help me find the words?"

"You don't need my help," Clayton said quietly. "It's not about specific words, it's about intention, and I don't think God would ever question your intention. Just say what comes naturally.

"I do want to caution you again, there is no guarantee that God will bring you the desired result. You have to hold on to the belief that God loves you and loves Tommy. But whatever His response is to your request for healing, you can be confident He'll give you the grace to face each step. In prayer we humble ourselves to acknowledge that God knows all things, and as our Creator, He truly understands the inner longings of our hearts. He'll do what He thinks best."

I started to protest, but Clayton touched my shoulder.

"Look, I know what you're going to say, that all you're praying for is Tommy's health and anything less than that is not acceptable. Well, God knows your feelings on that subject, but I think you're getting ahead of yourself. The prayers need to be offered up fervently—but with an open heart."

"Okay," I said. "Look, I know you've got stuff to do this morning, but maybe we'd better go out in the cold for a short run. I need to breathe, and I know I need to think."

"Well, bundle up, my boy," Clayton chuckled. "You said it was thirty degrees, but it's actually about fifteen, so cover your ears—not to God but to the cold."

"I get it," I said. "You never quit pitching."

"That's not quite right," he said. "The truth is, I don't ever quit believing."

chapter 20

As Tommy's suffering increased during the next few weeks of chemo, so did the intensity of my prayers, though I can't say I felt that God ever spoke to me directly. In retrospect, I think I was so angry watching my son battle for his life that, as Clayton said, my ears weren't open, and I have to admit neither was my heart.

Bridgette and I were both worn down as we alternated nights at the hospital, and for a couple who had always communicated about everything in our lives, we had become quiet, internal, and exhausted.

As winter began to give way to the wonder of New England spring, Clayton worked to keep my spirit up with longer weekend runs in preparation for the Boston Marathon.

Because everyone in my circle of friends and colleagues knew of Tommy's illness, it had not been difficult for me to raise money on behalf of palliative care for kids. In fact, without much effort from me, people's generosity had made the O'Connor family the leading fund-raising members of the marathon team that would be running Boston.

Bridgette had asked me if I really wanted to be doing something this taxing while trying to cope with Tommy's illness, Shannon's needs, and my job. The truth was it was in my morning runs with Clayton that I had my only moments of inner peace and solace. The physical effort required to do the long runs forced me to focus on something besides cancer; yet whenever I was tired, when the hills became tough, I was able to draw on my picture of Tommy going through so much pain and convert the thought into renewed determination: *I will complete this hill; I will complete this run; I will complete the marathon.* There were even days when I pushed the good pastor, though on paper he was a much better athlete than I was.

And so we lived in limbo, trying to help Tommy get through the ravages of his therapy and waiting in a state of virtual suspension for the next scans to reveal—what? We didn't know. We just had to hope.

It had become a painful habit, these meetings with Dr. Jennifer Hennessy, these conferences that would determine our family's future. I had come to appreciate our doctor's sincerity and her medical competence. When she had to pass on bad news, it was obvious that it hurt her deeply. She reflected it in the sound of her voice, in her manner, and in the way she communicated with Tommy.

I could tell Tommy had come to like Dr. Hennessy very much as well. Whenever she visited him she always knew what was happening with Boston sports teams. She understood early that mattered to Tommy. Through her work with other children, she had learned the ins and outs of the video games they loved. She even had taken the time to listen to the bands whose music meant something to the kids she treated. And then there were the Mini Snickers bars she always kept in her white coat pocket.

I had learned Dr. Hennessy was married to a pediatric cardiologist, and obviously their mutual interest in children's health provided them with a place for common understanding. They did not have children of their own—I didn't know why—but certainly Dr. Hennessy was compensating by providing an overflow of love for every child she tried to make well.

As with our first meeting months before, I sensed that there were other people in the room when we entered. The alarm bells began to go off in my head even before she started to speak.

"Mr. and Mrs. O'Connor, I've asked our team members to be present this morning, because we have some tough decisions to make."

I held my breath, and Bridgette took my hand.

"Tommy is not responding well to the chemo, and we are seeing greater metastasis in the lungs. I need to tell you that we are all very concerned."

I struggled to maintain control as I grasped at straws. "Okay, Doctor, but you told us that there are a number of drugs available that can—how did you put it?—outsmart the cells and stop the cancer. You did say that, didn't you?"

"Yes, I did, Mr. O'Connor, but I also explained that when we began Tommy's therapy we were using a blend of what seemed to be the best available with additional new medicines that had indicated possible success in early trials. Do you remember my saying that?"

"Yes, I remember," I said.

"Well then, let me explain again that what Tommy has been given in this round of chemo moved us more toward the experimental side—by that I mean medicines that were showing early promise of success. With the results not indicating improvement in Tommy's condition, we now need to talk about using completely experimental drugs."

"What does that mean?" Bridgette asked, her voice on the edge of breaking.

"It means," the doctor said carefully, "that Tommy's prognosis is not favorable, and we're trying our last resort medications to help him."

I had to ask the question, even though I already knew the answer. "Tommy is going to die. Is that what you're saying?"

It was the social services professional who answered the question. "Mr. O'Connor, no one can foresee the course of the disease, but it is the opinion of the team that we need to work together to make Tommy as comfortable as possible, both emotionally and physically."

"I don't understand," Bridgette said. "On the one hand you're telling us that there are still experimental drugs that might offer Tommy a cure, but you're also saying that it's time to make our son comfortable and to employ all of the services that the palliative care team can offer him."

Dr. Hennessy spoke again. "What we're saying is that as a family you have a tough decision to make. I am obligated to tell you that if we continue experimental chemo—though there is a possibility that it might benefit Tommy—we really are applying it to gain knowledge that could benefit other children. We still hope that Tommy will have a positive outcome—that he will live a little longer as a result."

Still trying to contain my emotion, I asked, "Okay, well, what about programs in other hospitals or treatments that are being offered outside the United States? Have you read about anything being used that is more than just experimental, I mean, that maybe hasn't been approved by the FDA but might help?"

"Mr. O'Connor," Dr. Hennessy said, "all of the hospitals in this country that treat children with cancer are linked. There's absolutely nothing happening at St. Jude's or MD Anderson or Mayo or Children's Hospital in Los Angeles that we're not trying here as well. We are all gaining the same information and sharing it. Now, there are countries in the world that are more open to experimentation without control than we are, but I have never had a patient utilize those outside sources and come out with a positive result."

"Well, we have to do something," Bridgette said, desperately. "We have to try anything that's out there to save Tommy, don't we?" Her question hung in the air. "Well, don't we?" she said again, challenging.

We were interrupted by a light tap on the door, and Rev. McRae walked in. "I'm sorry," he said, immediately sensing the mood in the room. "I'm very sorry to be late. I was with a family, and, well . . . I was with a family." His voice trailed off as he studied the faces of the people.

"I've just explained to the O'Connors," Dr. Hennessy said, "that Tommy's condition has worsened and that we are discussing experimental protocols for his continuing treatment."

McRae tried to offer a perspective. "As all of you know, I've had the chance to spend some quality time with Tommy, and I think maybe we are at the place when it's important to allow Tommy to participate in this decision."

"But he's only eleven," Bridgette said.

"Yes, but he's an old soul," McRae said gently, looking directly at Bridgette. "We see that a lot with these children. It's one of the things that seem to happen to kids as the disease progresses. They just get it. In so many ways I believe they do better than adults who face the same crises. Their awareness and innocence seem to create a capacity for acceptance. They see the truth clearly and handle it honestly. And when it comes to Tommy's comfort and future plans for his treatment, he should have a say about what he's willing to endure, understanding the limits of what treatment can ultimately do."

"So all of you believe we should ask Tommy what he wants to do?" I asked, not wanting any of this to happen.

"That is what we believe," Dr. Hennessy agreed. "In our experience as a care team, we have found that children should have the right to acknowledge their own destiny. It is the right of every human being. Would you like some time to think about this?" Dr. Hennessy asked quietly.

"No," Bridgette said. "I think we should talk to Tommy right away."

"Let me explain something else before we walk down the hall," Dr. Hennessy said. "Whether you as parents agree to either continue treatment or bring it to a halt, you provide us here at the hospital with your consent to a medical direction. You still hold the final decision, but we very much want the child, our patient, to agree to the choice we are all making. So let me ask you both: as parents, is it your desire to continue the treatment on an experimental basis?"

"Yes!" I said without hesitation. "Of course! Isn't that right, Bridgette? That's what we both want, isn't it?"

My wife, the love of my life, the mother of my children, spoke to me quietly, pulling the words from her heart. "I think," she said slowly, "that we should leave the decision in Tommy's hands and in God's."

"God, God, God!" I exploded. "I've been praying to God morning, noon, and night. Praying, asking, begging for Tommy's life, but He's not listening. We're all sitting here talking about this because we all know that God's not listening. Tommy is dying and God isn't hearing!"

I stood up with Bailey at my side. No one spoke as we moved

down the corridor. No one needed to. These good professionals were doing everything they could for Tommy and our family, and my outburst was the kind of thing they had undoubtedly heard many times before. Some of the team members peeled off, so as we moved into Tommy's room, Bridgette queried, stopping at the door, "Who will ask Tommy the question?"

"It's up to you," Dr. Hennessy said. "It can be me, Rev. McRae, or either of you."

"I'm going to ask him," I said, the anger still pouring out from inside. "I'll ask my son."

Opening the door, Bailey and I led the team into the room. Tommy was sitting up in bed when we came in, and I'm sure he sensed that something was up. I heard him turn his head against the pillows behind his neck, and I knew he was scanning our faces, trying to understand why we had all come in his room.

"Tommy," I began, having no idea how to even pose the life-and-death question. "Tommy, after a couple of weeks of rest, we want to try another kind of chemo to outsmart your cancer. Is that all right with you?"

I knew right away I wasn't asking the question fairly, unwilling to provide my son with the whole truth. But as Dr. Hennessy said, these children become wise old souls.

Tommy didn't hesitate. "You mean the cancer is getting worse, Dr. Hennessy? Because if you're trying something else, my cancer must be getting worse. Is that true?"

"Yes, Tommy," she said directly. "The tumor in your arms has spread to your lungs."

I felt sick, and Bridgette, who had been standing next to me, nearly fell as she swayed against my shoulder.

Tommy continued in a voice that seemed void of emotion,

"The drugs you want to use, Dr. Hennessy—have other children gotten well when they used these drugs?"

"A few," she said, "but these drugs are newer, and we haven't tried them on many people, so we really don't know how effective they are."

"I'm tired of being sick," Tommy said simply. "And I don't want to be sick anymore. I think I just want to go home."

And that was it. Tommy's decision had us packing up our son's stuff. We arranged with the palliative team to provide us with home care and the kind of hospice support necessary to make Tommy as comfortable as possible while we waited for God—the God I had come to hate—to provide the last chapter in the life of an eleven-year-old boy.

chapter 21

The feeling was surreal and yet oh so very real. My little boy, Tommy, was dying, and we were bringing him home because that's what he wanted. Yet on the surface there was an eerie sense of normalcy. The traffic was the same on the Southeast Expressway. Bailey greeted Tommy with a doggy enthusiasm that, despite the deathly serious nature of our arrival back in Scituate, made all of us laugh.

Shannon hugged her brother, and they held each other for what felt like forever. Tommy wanted to know how Shannon was doing in school, and rather than ask how he was feeling, his little sister wanted to talk about how comfortable her dolls were living in the house that her brother had completed for her on Christmas Eve.

Bridgette busied herself in the kitchen preparing dinner, and I didn't know what to do. The palliative care team professionals had told us to try to live in the now, not in the tomorrows but in the present, and also to celebrate what they called memory making, both for Tommy to create as a legacy and for us to be able to treasure forever.

Through the palliative care team, and now hospice, the volunteers were helping Tommy create a family tree with leaves and branches represented by pictures and funny stories or other important mementos, anything that said that a beautiful little boy had been here and made a difference to all who loved him.

As I sat in our living room on that first night listening to the normalcy around me, I kept trying to find the balance between acknowledging our situation as a family and planning—and this was the only way I could place it in my own head—the "make-a-wish" activities that might be meaningful to Tommy. I finally decided to talk to him about it, so as I tucked him in later that night I asked him what special things he might like to do.

"Opening day at Fenway," he said. "I want to see the Red Sox beat the Yankees."

"No problem," I told him. "We'll get box seats, maybe even meet some of the players."

"That would be great!" he said. "I really want to meet Josh Beckett because I love the way he pitches, and then there's Big Papi. Everybody loves Big Papi."

"Okay," I said, "I'll work on it. What else?"

"Well, I want to be at opening day for Little League and go out for pizza with everybody on the night of sign-ups."

"That's a great idea," I said, working to hold back tears. "I'm sure that all the team will be excited to see you."

"I wish I was pitching," Tommy told me. "We lost a lot of twelve-year-olds from last year's group, and I don't know if we're going to be as good this year."

"Well then, it seems to me that everybody will get a lot of inspiration when you show up."

Just then Bailey bounded into the room, having been outside for his nightly constitutional. Without asking permission he leaped up on Tommy's bed, making the boy laugh as he snuggled in close.

"I guess you've got a roommate," I said, smiling.

"Looks that way," Tommy said. "Is it okay, Dad?"

"You bet," I said, meaning it. "Bailey can stay here as much as he wants. Are you comfortable, Tommy?" I asked.

"I'm okay," he said.

"Are you having any pain?"

"Not much. Just a little bit in my arm."

"Well, call me if you need me. Okay? I'm always here for you."

I leaned down and kissed my son on the cheek and got licked for my trouble by Bailey, who wanted to be part of the love. I turned and walked out of Tommy's room, closing the door gently and losing it as I stood in the hall.

The reality was that I wouldn't always be there for Tommy, or rather he wouldn't always be here for us, and the sheer weight of that thought was much more than I was capable of handling.

We had not yet talked to Shannon about the serious nature of Tommy's cancer. I knew that would have to come, but it seemed to me that for now her joyous spirit would be even more positive than any medicine Tommy might be taking. So Bridgette tucked her in as usual, and we came together in the living room, a husband and wife looking for ways to talk to each other and gain the strength necessary to care for both of our children. For a little while we just sat holding each other, listening to make sure everything was settled upstairs.

I finally broke the silence. "Why, Bridgette? Why is this happening?"

My wife gave me an answer I should have suspected. "Only God knows that," she said. "Only God knows why He wants Tommy in heaven."

As in the hospital, I started to explode, but this time she touched my lips with her fingers.

"Look, Brian, there are things about living and dying, about pain and suffering, about many things in the world that seemingly have no answers. I understand that is very difficult for you to grasp, because you've always had to be so self-sufficient and determined. I knew right from the beginning of our marriage that faith was not really a part of your life, so there isn't any easy way for you to cope with what's happening to Tommy, but I did sense that your conversations with Rev. McRae were moving you toward considering the role that God can play in our lives."

I sighed, feeling guilty. "You know, Clayton really is a good man, and I probably should not have ranted at God the way I did in front of all of the team. They're such good people, and it amazes me that any of them are able to keep giving so much of themselves when you think about how hard it is for them to keep losing these kids most of the time."

"I don't know that's how they feel," Bridgette said, reflectively. "I think they believe that their work is very important and that they make a difference in all of the lives they touch."

"Well, there is no question about that," I said. "And I have really appreciated my time running with Clayton. It has been exciting to think about raising money to fight this disease."

"You know," she said, taking my hand, "you really should call him and apologize. I know how much he cares about you, and running the marathon is the right thing for you to do."

"I can't even think about that," I said. "Not now."

"Well, I heard Tommy talking to Shannon about it tonight," Bridgette said. "He's really proud of you, and he told his sister that he wanted to go to Boston to see you finish the race."

I shook my head, not convinced. "I'll call Clayton later.

Tommy told me how much he liked him, and that relationship will probably be important over the next few months."

I felt a chill run up my spine. Why couldn't I be saying "for the next few years" or "for the rest of Tommy's life" instead of only for a little while—for the shortest time—really, for no time at all? I put my head in my hands, rocking back and forth and crying softly. I heard Bridgette doing the same thing, and it brought me out of myself. I put my arms around my wife, and we sat there crying together quietly, working to accept what was to come.

The next morning, bright and early, I called Clayton. "Listen, pal," I said, "I just wanted to tell you how sorry I was for losing it the other day and taking all of those shots at God. I mean, it wasn't the right thing to do in front of you and your whole team."

"Oh, that's okay," he said. "We're used to it, Brian, and by the way, so is God. He understands that it's not easy to just accept everything that life doles out to us on—how should I put this?—on blind faith."

"Yeah. Well," I said, "this blind guy is probably as blind on the inside as he is on the outside. I just can't find a way to justify a loving God who could allow any of this to happen to a little boy—any little boy."

"As I told you before," McRae reiterated, "I feel that way sometimes too. But then I turn back to all of the things that God has done for me, and I become resigned to the things I just can't change. Look, this is a bit too heavy for a phone call, don't you think?"

"I agree with you," I said. "Tommy wants me to run the marathon—he told his sister that last night—so I suppose we'd better get back to work. We haven't been out on the roads for over a week."

"All right," he said. "With tomorrow being Saturday, how about maybe a fifteen-miler? What do you think?"

"I'll try it," I said, "and then maybe you could stay for breakfast and spend some time with Tommy?"

"Sure I could. That would be great."

"All right. I'll see you tomorrow."

I hung up, acknowledging again that Clayton was a kind and giving man, and as Bridgette said, we were lucky to have him in our lives.

And what about our lives? They seemed completely disjointed. When Tommy had a bad day, either because his arm was sore or because he was tired or because he was beginning to become short of breath, the reality of the disease weighed us down, driving our spirits into the ground. But then there were other days that were so alive and—dare I say it?—joyous.

The opening Monday of April in Fenway Park was an example. Through a guy in my office who knew the PR director of the Sox, the team rolled out the red carpet for us. Not only did Tommy meet his idols, Josh Beckett and David "Big Papi" Ortiz, but Terry Francona, the manager, had all kinds of memorabilia for Tommy to take home—hats and shirts, autographed balls, and even one of Big Papi's bats. Tommy even got to go out on the field during pregame batting practice and sit in the dugout with the team for a couple of innings, right next to the manager.

After the game we went into the clubhouse, and Tommy was made an honorary batboy for the day. Who says that athletes are selfish? These guys could not have been kinder to our eleven-year-old. And it wasn't just the Red Sox. We got the same kind of treatment at a Bruins game and with the Boston Celtics, where the Big Three—Paul Pierce, Ray Allen, and Kevin Garnett—autographed a basketball that Tommy slept with, making it difficult for Bailey to snuggle with him.

And that was another thing. Bailey would not leave Tommy's side whenever he was home. In fact, I had to force the dog to go to work with me. It was as if the big animal had first discovered Tommy's cancer, and now he was determined to love and take care of his young friend. The phenomenon of the way animals love is something I will never truly understand but will always appreciate.

In those months at home, Bailey was as important to Tommy as the hospice nurses, Dr. Hennessy, the volunteers, everyone in social service, and even Clayton, who made it a point to talk with Tommy after every one of our runs, sometimes for five minutes and other times for an hour. Generally I stayed out of the way, but I began to notice that Tommy referred to God more and more in his general conversations, usually thanking Him for a good day or sometimes asking Him to take away the pain when his right arm and shoulder were hurting.

Tommy's Little League team was scheduled to get together for a pizza party to celebrate the start of the season, and for three or four days before the event I sensed that my little boy was resting, gathering his strength, wanting to bring his best to the time with his teammates.

On the night of the party, Bridgette and I were surprised because Tommy came downstairs wearing his uniform from last year, even though it was falling off his emaciated frame.

"Why the uniform?" Bridgette asked.

Tommy's answer was simple. "Because I want them to know I'm still a member of the team," he said, "and because it makes me feel good to remember what it was like to be a pitcher."

When we arrived at Shakey's Pizza, our surprise continued. Tommy wanted pictures taken with every player on the team, and Bridgette was amazed, she told me later, at the way he hugged every friend. None of the kids seemed awkward as they embraced Tommy. They all knew he was very sick, yet his illness didn't stop them from openly caring about him and supporting him as a member of the team and, even more important, a friend they had missed a lot.

When we sat down for pizza, Tommy was completely involved in everybody's conversation. I heard them talking about sports and school and even about girls who had crushes on some of the guys. And to hear Tommy laugh, I mean really laugh out loud, touched my heart—yes, and even for a little while, lifted my spirits.

Tommy was a pepperoni pizza kid. He'd always loved it, and when Bridgette put a couple of big pieces on his plate he dove in, excited to eat it.

After four valiant attempts at swallowing, he quietly said to me, "I can't get it down, Dad. I mean, I guess I just don't really want it."

"That's okay, pal," I said. "I'm not very hungry either. For some reason it isn't very good tonight." I was lying, and we both knew it.

Later on when we got home, Tommy started upstairs and stopped on the landing. I heard the sound of his breathing and knew he was struggling.

"Let me help you," I said. "You're probably just a little tired. How about a piggyback the way we used to do when you were little?"

"No. That's okay, Dad," Tommy said, coughing with a wrenching sound that cut through me like a knife. "I just need to catch my breath."

And so we stood there on the landing, father and son, with Bridgette and Shannon watching from below, all of us, even Shannon, knowing that something had changed. The world had stopped turning. Spring wasn't coming. Hope had left the building, and Tommy had given his best on that last good day.

chapter 22

Just as day gives way to night and the brilliance of fall colors is replaced with the cold drabness of winter, hope had left the O'Connor house. Even the childlike optimism of little Shannon had been replaced by the devastation of tears—sobs that forced her to run to her mother's arms. We had tried to explain to her in the most basic way the concept of life and death, but Tommy's death—the brother she adored—was too much for this beautiful, innocent child to even begin to understand. What she did grasp was that she needed to be strong for her brother. Somehow she seemed to understand that all of us were about making Tommy's passage from this life—to what?—easier.

And what about Tommy himself—our eleven-year-old treasure who was dying? He had begun to withdraw into himself. He talked with us less and less, and as he became immobile, confined to a wheelchair or his bed, and the rasping in his lungs became audible, Tommy seemed to be readying himself to cross over. Or maybe he was applying what limited energy he had left only to the things where it was needed.

Whenever Clayton would come into the house with me at the

end of a morning run, Tommy seemed to perk up. He seemed to look forward to the minister's stories and private conversation. Bridgette and I did not interfere, and when I asked on the day after one of these meetings what Clayton and Tommy had talked about, my friend simply said, "It's up to Tommy. I don't think I should break his confidence."

And so that's where we were, as Clayton and I ran toward the lighthouse on an early spring morning.

"Tommy had a rough night," I said. "Dr. Hennessy told us that we are getting to the time when he will have to be on oxygen. It's the lung metastasis that's killing him."

"I know," he said. "Dr. Hennessy called me in yesterday to brief me on Tommy's condition in case there were things . . . " and he stopped.

I continued the thought. "In case there were things that you needed to talk about with him, to wrap up, to put a bow on Tommy's life. Is that what you mean, Clayton?" Right away I felt horrible about what I had just said to this good man who had become my friend.

He shrugged off my insult. "Well, there are things that are important to talk about," he said. "I want you to know that I'm not driving the conversation. It's Tommy who's asking the questions, and I will tell you, Brian, some of what he's asking I just don't have answers for. Frankly, nobody does."

"Well, I've got one for you," I said, taking a deep breath as we arrived at the top of the hill and turned to run along the cliff above the ocean. "Can you give me any explanation, either supported by the Bible or just out of your own head, as to why some people are healed and others are not? Is it just random? I mean, genetics, physical breakdown? Or is God involved in the decision as to who lives and who dies and when?"

I heard my friend take a deep breath. "We've hit another one of those moments when I have absolutely no idea. There are some people Jesus encounters who are healed, and frankly, there are others who ask for His healing presence and are not made whole. There doesn't seem to be any logic in this, and when you read Scripture you can't help but say to yourself, *I hope I'm one of the ones*—boy, and this is a difficult word—*who is* favored *by His healing hand.* But we are in a conundrum because the bottom line is you have to ask. You just have to ask."

"What do you think I've been doing, Clayton? I've been praying, I've been asking, I've been begging. Tommy's been asking, and I know Bridgette and Shannon have been praying. And you've been praying. But Tommy's much worse. There is no hope."

I came to a sudden stop in the run and dropped my head into my hands, not able to hold back the sobs that wracked my body. My friend waited patiently.

Eventually he said, "You have to believe in God's love, Brian, and allow Tommy to be wrapped in that love. Tommy's circumstances don't make sense to any of us, but Tommy has decided that God loves him. Now, I'm not trying to tell you that he completely understands the concept of life and death and has balanced it with his newfound faith in God, but I'm pretty sure that all kids go through the cancer experience finding security when they break their faith down to a simple truth. And that truth is God loves us—each and every one of us."

"Look," I said, "you've been telling Tommy stories. Are there any of them that you've found that can apply to this conversation? Because if there is, I need to hear about them too."

For a while my friend was quiet. "Well," he said, "there is the story of Jairus' daughter."

"Okay, go on."

"Well, it's a story about a father just like you, worried about his child, who comes forward and interrupts Jesus, not only because he is a concerned father, but he's the kind of guy who's been at odds with Jesus from the very beginning.

"You see, this man represents the religious tradition that Jesus seems to pay very little attention to. So you get the sense that in this moment of grave danger to his child, in absolute complete humility, he puts all of the crap aside and comes to Jesus and says, 'Lord, my little daughter is extremely sick. Please come and lay hands on her.' Because he's already seen, as many people had, that when Jesus lays hands on someone, they get better. And the great news is that without equivocation or an 'I told you so,' and with no theological exam required, Jesus simply says, 'Okay. Let's go.'

"They turn, and as they take just the first three or four steps, there is a woman in the crowd who had been bleeding for twelve years, the story says. The connection is that Jairus' daughter is twelve years old. Now, this woman has been bleeding for as long as this little girl has been alive, and we're told that the woman had exhausted her resources. All of her options were gone. Now, if it was today I think we'd say that she had tried to get insurance to cover her problem but couldn't. She's seen as many doctors as possible, even mortgaged her house and gone broke trying to solve her problem. She maybe even has tried cults or witch doctors. I don't know, but the point is she's out of choices.

"So she says to herself, 'If I can just touch the hem of His garment,' meaning Jesus, 'I'll be well again.' Now, is that faith? I guess so, because when she does, Jesus stops and says, 'Who touched me?' The people around him look at him like he's crazy, but Jesus is sure that he's been touched, and so He looks through the crowd and sees the woman. She's lying on the ground. She has fallen after getting to Jesus. And right there He says, 'My daughter, your faith has made you well. Go in peace.'

"Hardly had Jesus engaged in this moment—a very tender moment—when these idiots come running up from the guy's house and they say, 'Don't bother to come, Jesus. Jairus' daughter is dead.' Now, if you're Jairus, what would you think? I mean, wouldn't you rail against that?

"Imagine the loneliness that Jairus is feeling now. While Jesus took the time to heal this woman, Jairus' own daughter died. The delay cost him his daughter's life. There can't be an emptier moment for a parent. While Jairus is trying to figure all of this out, Jesus grabs him by the arm and says, 'We're going anyway.'

"Brian, that's what I think God does with all of us. When you feel like something can't get any worse, God is there. 'Let's go right know,' Jesus says. So they walk to the house, and people there are already beginning to mourn. They can hear the wailing blocks before they arrive. As they work their way through the crowd, Jesus looks at these people and says, 'Get out of here, you noisemakers. She's not dead. She's just sleeping.' And they look at Him again like He's crazy. And He says to Jairus and the mother, 'Don't doubt. Believe.' He takes them into the bedroom and holds the little girl's hand and says, 'Get up. It's time to rise.' And the story says she opened her eyes and walked out.

"All I know is that for her it worked. For that father, his prayer was answered. Is that going to happen for you? I don't know. But I don't think any of us should let Tommy go to God without asking."

I worked to control my frustration. "Okay, two people asked and two people were healed. Isn't that God being selective? How is anyone to interpret selectivity as anything loving?"

"I don't think you can," my friend said.

I was angry now. "You told me to pray! I've been praying, nonstop, morning, noon, and night in the way you taught me. The Our Father, all of it. Look, Clayton, I'm at max praying. If Tommy dies, what is this thing you call faith or religion worth if it's selective? It's worse than anything man can ever do to man."

"Again," Clayton said, sighing between strides, "I admit it, Brian. I don't have a helpful answer. All I can say is that as I pray, there is no doubt of the 'I am with you always' commitment of God to us. That's His answer to every prayer: 'I'm with you, holding you, embracing you, surrounding you. I'm here.' God is with Tommy, and there is a presence with you, even if you don't plug into it, with me, with Bridgette, with Shannon, and it can only be felt by those willing to ask in faith. And that piece of the mystery I'm absolutely sure of.

"Now, look, we'd all like it to be wrapped in a nice package, but there just is no formula to the liturgy, to the lessons we're supposed to learn. There is no 'do this and that will happen' structure in God's love. God just doesn't work that way. That's truly all I know—all I can be sure of."

Again I was on the edge of tears, but this time they were tears of anger and frustration, so I ran faster, trying to run away from the reality of Tommy's pending death, trying to escape the pain that tore at my gut.

Eventually we slowed and I said, "Could it be my prayers? I mean, are they too stiff, too structured? Maybe I'm not praying the right way."

"I've told you before, Brian," Clayton said, "there is no right way to pray. Look, I'm praying in the same way you are. My prayers for Tommy are full of tears, anger, fumbling, doubt, laser focus, bewilderment, helplessness, and hope. Look, just as there's no formula for answers, there's no right way to pray. You need to extend some kindness to yourself. Don't waste energy on the form of prayer. God's listening if your prayers are coming from a place of true love and faith. It's that simple. The words you choose are irrelevant. It is your broken heart that prompts God to love you and listen. It's in the basic honesty of a broken heart that causes God to pay attention and hopefully provides you with real inner peace.

"Look, I don't know that this is of any comfort to you, Brian," Clayton said as we came to a stop just outside my house, "but I believe there will be a day for you and me, and I don't know when for Tommy, when we will each take our last breath, and if we want him to, God will embrace us and provide us with a life beyond our capacity to understand because we will be so filled with His presence and His perfect love."

Quietly I said, "And that's heaven?"

Clayton hugged me as we stood at the end of the driveway. "That's heaven," he said quietly. "It's God's promise to all who believe."

chapter 23

Now it was all about watching and waiting.

The hospice staff was doing a spectacular job attending to Tommy's needs. Thanks to Dr. Hennessy's caring wizardry, our son did not seem to be in much pain, and she seemed to have found the balance between medicating him enough to keep him comfortable and not closing off those moments of lucidity that allowed us those oh-so-meaningful experiences of communication.

Though Tommy sometimes sat up in his wheelchair, most of his time was spent in a hospital bed brought in by the hospice and placed in our living room.

Bridgette told me that Tommy seemed to really focus his gaze on our faces, most particularly Shannon's, and on Bailey, who never left his side. I literally had to drag the dog out to relieve himself. He was completely focused on Tommy, and he was gentle to the extreme when the boy reached out periodically to pat him.

Each day Tommy would rally his strength to complete tasks that seemed to be critically important to him, such as his memory collage of pictures that put his eleven years in perspective. And one afternoon, he really took me back.

"Dad," he said, "I've made a list."

"Of what?" I asked, not understanding.

"Of all my stuff and who it should go to," he said, "when I'm—"

I interrupted. "Don't say that, Tommy."

"When I'm dead," he went on, almost matter-of-factly. "I want the things that matter to go to people I love." He continued, very organized. "I want all my baseball stuff to go to members of my team. My glove should go to Danny Murphy because he's the starting pitcher this year. The Big Papi bat, Chad Daniels should have that because he's going to be hitting cleanup for the team. And the autographed baseballs we got from the Red Sox should go to Eddie Martin, because he's the worst player on the team, and the balls will make him feel good."

"Tommy," I said quietly, working to hold back the tears, "you're the most amazing son any father could ever have."

Along with the generosity Tommy expressed with his friends was a sensitivity: he did not want any of them to visit, because he said that he didn't want to make any of them sad. I believe what he really was saying was that the concept of death was much too heavy for any eleven-year-olds who didn't have to deal with it directly.

Later that night, I was helping Bridgette with the dishes following the evening meal. From the living room I heard a conversation that nearly made me drop a serving plate on the floor.

Tommy was saying, "Don't worry, Shannon, when I'm up in heaven, I'll be watching you all the time."

"You mean you'll be my angel?"

"Sure," Tommy said. "You'll be the only one of all your friends who has her own angel up there in heaven to take care of you."

"But I want you right here all the time. Right here with me."

They must've hugged because the conversation ended.

At night we got in the habit of operating in shifts, with one of us in the armchair next to Tommy's bed and the other trying to get a few hours of needed sleep.

Bridgette was on watch, and I was dreaming.

In my dream Tommy was grown up, and Bridgette, Shannon, and I were sitting in box seats in Fenway Park as our adult Tommy pitched the seventh game of the World Series against the Dodgers. I heard the catcher's glove pop and the umpire call strike three. The Sox had won and Tommy was a hero.

My vision of a future that could never be was interrupted by Bridgette shaking me awake.

"What is it?" I said, jolted back to reality. "Is it Tommy? What's going on?"

"I know it's the middle of the night," she said, "but for some reason Tommy wants to see Clayton. I don't understand, but he seems to feel really strongly about it."

I threw on my bathrobe and slippers and went downstairs. Tommy's breathing was raspy, and his speech came slowly, but I could tell his thoughts were clear and focused.

"Dad," he said, "can you get Rev. McRae to come here now?"

"It's the middle of the night, Tommy," I said gently. "He's probably asleep."

"I know," my son said, "but I need to talk to him now. Right now."

The tone in Tommy's voice made his urgency very clear. I picked up the phone in the kitchen and dialed my friend.

"Hello?" the sleepy voice said.

"Clayton, it's Brian. I don't know why, but Tommy says he needs to see you right now."

The preacher didn't even question it. "I'll be there in thirty minutes," he said. "Tell Tommy I'll be right there."

Over the next half hour we were all quiet, and I got the feeling that Tommy was trying to rest, focusing his strength for the conversation that must have been critically important.

When Clayton arrived, he pulled up a chair next to Tommy's hospital bed and took my son by the hand. This time Bridgette and I remained in the room, standing together at the end of the bed.

The oxygen made a hissing sound as Tommy fought for breath, but when he spoke his voice was clear, and his question was right to the point. "Rev. McRae," he said, "is there really a heaven? I really need to know."

I heard the ticking of the grandmother clock in the far corner of our living room and realized that Clayton's answer was not immediate.

Why is he hesitating? I thought, as the clock continued to tick. *Isn't that the centerpiece of what he believes?*

Finally he answered, sounding uncomfortable but committed. "Yes, there is a heaven, Tommy, and the reason I know that—in fact, let me say it differently—the reason I believe that is because when I read the Bible and I see a great kid like you, I know that God wants to hold all of us in His loving arms.

"You know, Tommy, the Bible talks about heaven, but it doesn't tell us too much about what it's going to be like. Parts of the Bible talk about heaven being a place where there are no tears. I really like that. And we always hear about how much love there is in heaven. And we all want that. And the most important thing, Tommy, is that heaven is the place where God is and where everyone who God loves will share it with Him. It's such a happy place we can't really imagine it, and it's there for all of us."

"What will dying be like?" Tommy asked.

Clayton thought for a minute. "Nobody knows exactly. But let me try and explain it this way. Have you ever been to the circus?"

"Yes," Tommy said, struggling to breathe. "We went last year."

"Well," Clayton went on, "do you remember the flying trapeze? How the girl would swing out into space and let go of the bar?"

"Yeah," Tommy said. "It was really scary."

"That's right," Clayton said. "It was scary for you to watch, but it wasn't scary for the trapeze artist because she was sure that the man on the other side would catch her. She was absolutely sure that she would never fall because his arms were strong and he would take care of her. That's the way it is with God. And the thing is, Tommy," Clayton continued, leaning closer, "God will never let go of us. Once we're in His hands in heaven, we're safe forever. Nothing bad will ever happen to us again, because God will always hold us in His love."

Tommy asked, "Will we know each other in heaven? Will we be just like we are right here on earth?"

"I believe heaven is a place where we all know each other."

Tommy asked, "Well, do you think we'll have the same bodies when we're in heaven? I mean, will I be a little boy and will Dad be blind?"

I choked back tears and Bridgette squeezed my hand.

"Well, the Bible tells us that we'll have different bodies when we're in heaven, but it really doesn't describe the bodies we'll have. I do know this, Tommy," Clayton said with real commitment in his voice. "I do know that when you're in heaven, there will be no more cancer, no more pain. I know that because it's God's promise."

"What do you think we'll be doing in heaven?" Tommy asked, laboring to breathe.

"One thing the Bible tells us is that in heaven we'll be praising God with the angels. That sounds pretty cool, right?

"Angels are real?"

"Yes, they're very real. The Bible tells us that there are lots of angels in heaven, and I suppose they're beings a lot like you and me, created by God. Angels have the privilege and the fun of being very close to God. They get to hang around with God."

"I've never seen an angel," Tommy said.

"Most of us haven't," Clayton answered, "but I believe that the angels are always watching out for us, hoping that we make the right decisions, and they want us to join them someday in heaven, sharing in the kingdom.

"Let me say it this way, Tommy. I believe that the angels are God's proof that He is always here for us."

"If I go to heaven," Tommy asked with real concern in his voice, "will I know what Mom and Dad and Shannon are doing down here?"

"I think so," Clayton said. "I'm pretty sure that that's something God allows."

Bridgette couldn't help herself. She leaned down, kissing Tommy gently and telling him how much she loved him. I joined her, not fighting my tears, and Clayton respectfully waited.

"I'm afraid to die," Tommy said.

I heard Bridgette's intake of breath, but in that horrible moment Clayton was terrific. He said gently, "I'm a lot older than you, and I'm pretty scared to die too. We all feel that way because nobody knows exactly how to do it or what will happen. But what I'm sure of is that God will catch us when we swing across the separation between this life and the next. I know that God will not let us fall. He loves us too much. And Tommy," Clayton added, "Jesus was very clear about this when he was here on earth. He said, 'I am with you always.' He is as near as your breath, as close as your heart. So when we're going to cross over into heaven, even though we don't know exactly how it happens, Jesus is right there to guide us and keep us safe until God holds us close."

"Thank you, Rev. McRae," Tommy said. "Thank you for telling me about heaven. It does sound like a pretty cool place."

"Better than you can imagine," Clayton said. He sounded exhausted.

Tommy sighed. "I think I'd like to sleep for a while. I'm really tired."

"That would be good," Bridgette said as she pulled the quilt tighter around Tommy's shrunken frame.

"I'll be right back, pal," I told my son. "I'll just walk Clayton out to his car."

"Good night, Tommy," Clayton said, stepping back from the bed. "Have a good rest."

"Good night," Tommy said, already sliding into sleep.

I walked outside with my friend, hearing the night sounds of crickets and frogs coming from the marsh down by the lighthouse.

"Thank you," I said. I didn't know what else to say. "Thank you, Clayton. I know Tommy really appreciated you coming, and so did Bridgette and I."

"I know he's scared," my friend said. "None of us really knows how to die and cross over. There's no class for it or formula. We just have to take it on faith."

"But you're sure?" I said, really asking for the first time. "You're sure about God? About heaven? About His love?"

The minister put his arm around my shoulders. "I am as sure as any mortal man can be," he said quietly, "because I believe in what God has told us again and again. I believe in the Scriptures, and I've seen enough people make the passage from this side to the other to know that heaven really is out there."

We hugged, and Clayton got into his car and drove away.

I stood still for a while in the darkness, weighed down by the inevitable truth that our beloved Tommy was going to die sooner rather than later. Yet I was buoyed by the thought that there just might be something more on the other side. I knew that's what Bridgette believed. It was certainly what Rev. McRae believed. But now, most important, I understood that it was what Tommy believed, and that was the truth that really mattered.

chapter 24

It didn't matter to any of us that New England was offering a remarkable spring. For the first time in my life the smells of fresh cut grass, the ground opening, first roses, and my beloved ocean didn't matter. My senses were sending information to a brain incapable of absorbing anything but death.

The hospice nurse was visiting Tommy twice a day now, and the social workers were discussing how to cope with grief and how to prepare for . . . We were coming to the end, and all of us knew it. So Bridgette and I were no longer sleeping in shifts but dozing in our armchairs at the side of Tommy's bed.

Upstairs, Bridgette's mother had returned to occupy Shannon, although our daughter was almost as intense about her time with Tommy as we were—preferring to be with him every day after school.

Even through his heavy medication, now and then Tommy seemed to focus and snap back into life. What made these moments odd was that often he would begin a conversation as if we had already been having it. For example, at the suggestion of the hospice support team, I would turn on the television when the Red Sox were playing, in the hopes that Tommy would take an interest. It might be the sixth inning when I realized that Tommy was awake, yet he would talk about something that happened back in the third, making me understand that, though he wasn't always communicating in a verbal sense, he was paying close attention.

In one of these moments, with the Sox leading 3–2 over the Tigers, he said, "Dad, I want to go to heaven with my Little League uniform on."

"You what?" I said, taken back.

"I want you to make sure that I have my uniform on when it's time for me to go to heaven."

"Okay," I said. "I'll remember. Hey, Tommy, I'll be right back. I just need to use the bathroom, okay?"

I went upstairs so my son wouldn't hear me and threw up, crying at the same time. He had seemed definite and so matter of fact when he told me he wanted to go to heaven with his uniform on. It was as if Tommy had come to terms with his destiny, while we—those who would be left behind—could not even bear discussing it.

At another moment I heard him talking to his sister about heaven. He emphasized to Shannon that they would be together forever when it was her time to join him in heaven, and while she was down here on earth, he would be keeping an eye on her. It was more than I could cope with, and Bridgette, the mother of this brave little boy, was just as devastated.

While the hospice nurse was making sure that Tommy's medications were correct at the end of an afternoon, we stepped outside to breathe some fresh air.

"Tommy said that he wants to go to heaven in his Little League uniform," I told Bridgette.

"I know," she said. "When you were dozing he mentioned it to me twice. He also wanted to know why you haven't been running the last few days."

"What do you mean?" I asked.

"Well, it seems that our Tommy has decided that it's very important for you to raise money for other children with cancer and complete the Boston Marathon."

"I'm not going to—"

"Oh, yes, you are," she said. "You're going to run the marathon, and you're going to run it great because it matters to Tommy."

I didn't answer my wife. I couldn't even think about a marathon now, and yet, as always, I was touched to my core at the idea that Tommy was thinking about helping other children with this disease as his own life was ebbing away.

When we returned to the house, Tommy seemed to be asleep, and the hospice nurse, a lovely Irish lady named Ginny Callahan, motioned to Bridgette and me to step back outside.

This is it, I thought. *We're about to get the word that Tommy's death is imminent.*

Nurse Callahan was gentle but definite. "It won't be long," she said. "Tommy's vital signs have reached the critical point. It could be anytime now."

Bridgette silently turned and walked into the house.

"Where are you going?"

"I'm calling the priest for last rites," she said, "and then I'm calling Clayton."

"I already called him," Nurse Callahan said. "He's on his way down from Boston."

"Thank you," I said. "Thank you very much."

I realized that I had not been considering Bridgette's Catholicism because of my involvement with Clayton McRae. I guess it just didn't dawn on me that my wife's faith also needed to be part of the equation.

After calling the monsignor at St. Mary's Catholic Church, she came back outside and took my hand. "I want a Mass for Tommy," she said, "but I explained to Father Riley that we want Clayton to do the homily. Is that all right with you?"

"Sure," I said. "I think that's what Tommy would want. In fact, I know that's what he would want."

The hours dragged by. The oxygen hissed and Tommy struggled to breathe. He had not communicated with us all day, and I began to wonder if he would ever speak to us again.

Bridgette's father had arrived, and so had Clayton McRae. Ginny Callahan was with us, and Dr. Hennessy had called a number of times to see if there was anything she could do.

Bridgette and I held Tommy's hands, and Shannon hovered at the top of the bed watching over her brother. Occasionally Clayton read aloud from Psalms in the hopes that they might comfort Tommy.

It was Shannon who noticed when Tommy's eyes blinked open. "Tommy?" she said. "Tommy?"

"Hi, Shannon," he said, sounding just like himself. "Are you okay?"

"I love you, Tommy," she said, simply.

I felt Tommy take his hand away from mine, and with a tremendous effort of will he reached up and pulled his sister toward him. Their tears mingled as they kissed good-bye.

"Rev. McRae," Tommy said, looking directly at the minister. "I saw them."

"That's wonderful, Tommy," Clayton said, as if he expected just such a comment from our little boy.

"You saw who?" Bridgette asked, not understanding. "Who did you see, Tommy?"

"The angels," Tommy said, "and they told me not to be afraid. They said they're waiting for me and they'll take care of me until all of us are together again in heaven."

Nobody spoke; nobody moved. Tommy seemed suspended somewhere between heaven and earth, both worlds touching him. In this moment of terrestrial vision and faith—Tommy's faith—none of us, even Clayton McRae, knew what to do or what to say. Tommy slipped back into that semiconscious state that we believed still allowed him to hear us, and so we took turns telling him how much we loved him—kissing him and making him understand that there would never be a moment when we wouldn't be thinking of him and making him a part of our lives here on earth.

At some point, I don't know how long after his visitation from the angels, death came quietly for our little boy. In a small sigh of peaceful resignation, Tommy was gone.

The others moved silently out of the bedroom while Bridgette and I held Shannon and cradled Tommy's head in our hands. I touched his face with my fingertips, hoping that a life of blindness would allow me to absorb Tommy's every feature and texture, transferred from my loving touch directly into my brain.

"God," I silently prayed, caressing my child's cheek, "please, God, let my hands hold the memory so that I can touch him every day and draw him to me in the long, sleepless nights that I know will be a constant in my life."

As I turned, the tears pouring down my face, I was surprised by a sound so chilling that no one in the house ever forgot it. Though Tommy's death came peacefully enough, Bailey's grief, his animal awareness, reminded us of the loss everyone was feeling. This great dog, whose training restricted his barking overtly, stood in the doorway of Tommy's room with his head cocked facing the sky and keened, announcing his grief.

Someone called the funeral home, and sometime later Tommy's body was taken away to be prepared for burial, dressed in his Little League uniform, ready to meet his God.

More family arrived, including my father and sisters. As in my childhood, communication with my family was difficult, yet there is a comfort gained by having family around you at moments like this. Though gaps would always exist between the O'Connors, they were narrowed by the shared embraces and the understanding that we loved each other.

chapter 25

It was raining on the morning we left the funeral home and accompanied the hearse bearing Tommy's body to St. Mary's Catholic Church in Scituate Harbor. The rain reminded me of all the
tears shed during the three days between the time Tommy went to
God and this cold New England morning.

I was amazed that the church was completely full. In his
eleven short years, Tommy had touched so many lives—far more
than I ever knew. His Little League teammates were there, along
with classmates and their parents, teachers, and many of the hospital personnel that Tommy had come into contact with during
his year at Dana-Farber.

The Mass as celebrated by Father Riley was beautiful, and when
the "Ave Maria" was sung by a wonderful tenor who gave his best, I
found that the rituals of Catholicism that had been so much a part
of my early life were comforting and, yes, even reassuring.

When it was Clayton's turn to deliver a homily, he came to the
altar and stood quietly for a moment, looking out at the assem-
blage of mourners and gathering his thoughts.

Then he asked us to join him in prayer. "Lord, we ask that we might be renewed this day. Broken places made whole. Dead places come alive. Empty places filled with Your Holy Spirit. We want that for all of us who come here to celebrate the life of Thomas Joseph O'Connor, who left us too soon but now resides in the loving arms of God, and so we ask God to stir the Holy Spirit in all of us. We ask this in His holy name. May the words of my mouth and the meditations of our hearts be acceptable in Thy sight, oh, Lord, our strength and redeemer, Amen.

"We are gathered in this holy place to celebrate the life of Thomas Joseph O'Connor, born April 14, 1997, died April 10, 2009. We are able to celebrate that life because, though death may end our physical lives, it does not end in any way our relationships because nothing truly dies if it's remembered, and the memories of Tommy O'Connor will live in the hearts of everyone in this church today.

"And so on this day and the days to come, we have the privilege of remembering Tommy's life. We celebrate that life by allowing those qualities Tommy exhibited to become a part of our own character, to embrace his spirit, his joy, his love as part of who we are as human beings. For many of us who weren't there at the beginning of Tommy's journey, imagine how Brian and Bridgette felt when they held their baby for the first time and counted ten fingers and ten toes; when they became aware of his first smile, heard his first words, shared in his first steps and all the steps to come; the early triumphs of a toddler and the constant joy they experienced with every child's basic questions: 'Why?' 'Why are things the way they are?' 'What does it all mean?'

"What I want us to think about, each of us in our own way, is that we were fortunate enough to bear witness to Tommy's becoming the Tommy we've known. Those of you who taught him in the classroom or became his friend on the playground or the Little League field, you watched and shared as he enriched your life with the uniqueness that was and is Tommy O'Connor.

"We ask how cancer could happen to someone with so much promise. Many of you have lived the pain of this wonderful family, as I see his doctors here in attendance and the nurses who cared for him. We know that over the last year there have been so many moments of hope that were dashed as the cancer progressed.

"And what was the constant in all of this? Tommy's courage, the way he rallied his spirits to fight the good fight. Tommy was more accepting than many adults of the realities he faced. He understood when the fight was too much. He understood that there came a time when it became more important for him to prepare to go to his God than to remain in pain here with us.

"We talked a lot about those things, Tommy and I, and I want to say to all of you assembled here that Tommy was crystal clear about his faith in God, his trust in Jesus, and yes, his belief in resurrection. On the last night Tommy spent on earth, he spoke to his mother, his father, his sister, and me as we stood at his bedside. He told us that the angels had visited him and that he was not afraid, that they would accompany him to heaven and there he would be embraced by God's love.

"When we look at Tommy's life, we should remember not only the tender ending but also the memories that allow us to always keep him with us in our hearts. His was a short life well lived.

"My friends, it is our privilege now to give him to God. There are a lot of us in this church, myself included, who would say, 'No! I can't let go. I won't let go of Tommy. He belongs to us!' And I understand that, most particularly for Brian, Bridgette, and Shannon O'Connor, what I'm suggesting may seem impossible. *Haven't we already given him up?* they're thinking. *Haven't we sacrificed enough at the loss of our son and brother? Isn't that enough?*

"Tommy knows that holding on to him can never help us. It will not relieve our pain. So as difficult as this is, we need to say, 'I'm working this morning to let go of Tommy O'Connor.' How can we do less, believing that he is in that better place, that he is with the angels and in the arms of God? That Tommy is in a place where there are no tears, no pain, no cancer, and no death?

"What about resurrection? How does it help us in the struggle to understand Tommy's passing? And is it truly God's promise, his guarantee of a life beyond the capacity of human understanding?

"Here we are in April—the Easter season—and we are seeing the promise of spring fulfilled. Winter ends. Flowers bud and bloom. The air takes on a softness as it changes from winter's chill. This spring into life for all of us seems natural, but the concept of resurrection—that feels so unnatural because today in this church most of us feel that everything has ended right here. Tommy, the boy we loved, is gone. Springtime will never come to his grave. That's what we know. That's what we expect. That certainly was what Mary Magdalene was thinking the first Easter morning.

"John tells us that the Sabbath was over as Mary made the long walk to Jesus' tomb. As her eyes adjusted to the early light she realized that someone had moved the stone. John says she ran and brought back two others with her so that they too could see. In fact, once they had seen and satisfied themselves that what she said was true, they left her there weeping.

"Mary stayed rooted to the last place where she knew Jesus with no idea what to do next. Even the angels couldn't soften her sadness. They were there, Scripture says. 'Why are you weeping?' they asked her. 'They've taken away my Lord,' she answered. 'And I don't know where they've taken Him.' Then she turned and bumped into the gardener, and she pressed her question to him. 'If you've carried him away, where have you taken him?'"

I heard Clayton move out from behind the podium, coming closer to the mourners, as if he were the questioner.

"But at that wondrous moment she heard the voice of Jesus, and she recognized it when He simply called her by name: 'Mary.' She turned and cried, 'My teacher!'

"Jesus then gave Mary the word that I want to give to you. Jesus said to Mary, 'Do not hold on to Me because I am not yet ascended to My Father.' He probably could hear in her voice that she wanted him to remain here on earth with her as He was, but He was very clear: 'Don't hold on to Me.'

"We want life to go back to the way it was, with Tommy O'Connor happy, healthy, and pitching a perfect game. But that is not what God wants for us. God wants us to let go and believe in the resurrection made possible by Jesus, our ascent into heaven to be with Him always.

"I know the idea of another life can be frightening, and Tommy and I talked about that. He told me that he was afraid to die, and I told him that that was true for all of us. But Tommy has given us a remarkable gift because he told us, as directly as Jesus told Mary, that the angels came and that he was not afraid, knowing that they would take care of him. Not since Jesus and the resurrection has a case for heaven been more clearly stated than by an eleven-year-old boy full of innocence and God's love. Tommy is our teacher. Tommy is like the Holy Spirit because, through his courage and his love, he has pointed us to the pathway to eternal life.

"This morning we celebrate Tommy's life and the nobility of his passing. Tommy is a light that allows us to have a glimpse into the mysteries that have challenged man since the beginning of time, the mysteries of life and death, and yes, the promise of resurrection and a life to come."

It would take me time to understand the power of Clayton McRae's sermon on the morning of my son's funeral. Time would need to pass before the pain of grief could turn to the joy of memory.

As we left the church and drove to the cemetery, the sun burst through the clouds. "Look! There's a rainbow!" Shannon said, the surprise clear in her voice. "There's a rainbow, Dad, and Tommy's painting it just for us."

chapter 26

The emotional landscape for the O'Connor family was as bleak as an Antarctic winter. We lived. That was all any of us could say. I think we ate. We may have slept, though time had no pattern. Day, night, work, school, friends, neighbors—all of it melded into a vapid emptiness with no relief.

Tommy was gone, and the hole in our hearts, minds, and souls was a chasm that could never be filled. We were wooden in our day-to-day routine. I think I went to the office. I believe Bridgette took Shannon to school and kept the house. And Shannon—what about little Shannon? She was consumed by her loss. She held on to us, trying to find a path that would once again open her up to giving and accepting love. And in her efforts we were forced to rouse ourselves out of our malaise and offer her something in return. It was small in those early days, like the smallest song of a sparrow, the first bud of spring, the tiniest breath of hope.

And I suppose that's what Clayton McRae knew.

I began to receive phone calls or visits where he said, "Hey, bud, the marathon is in two weeks." "You have twelve days to get ready." "Ten days from now we're going to be there in Hopkinton running the race for Tommy."

And somehow that idea, to run for Tommy, prompted me to join my friend and go on some short morning jogs to awaken the muscles, even if the spirit seemed dead. We didn't speak much on those runs. We were just together, communing in silence.

On our last light five-miler four days before Boston, Clayton finally said, "You know, Brian, you're doing the right thing, this race for Tommy. It's what he wanted. I don't think you could find a better way to pay tribute than to allow Tommy's legacy to be loving and caring for other children."

"I know," I said, still stiff in my response, "but I don't have it in me. I just can't seem to find the strength. Even now, all I want to do is cry."

And so there we were on the third Monday of April, Patriots' Day, standing on the starting line in Hopkinton, twenty-six miles from Copley Square and the finish line of the Boston Marathon.

The race is more than a hundred years old, and it winds from Hopkinton through Asheville, Framingham, Wellesley, Newton, and eventually into the city of Boston, where thousands greet the runners.

The race begins downhill. In fact, during the first mile the elevation drops 133 feet, and the danger is being trampled by the pounding herd full of adrenaline and purpose. Clayton did a masterful job guiding me through the crowd. I remember I held on to his elbow and measured the rhythm of his steps, trying to keep my own feet from tangling with my friend's.

By the 5K mark it was easier, and since the first twelve miles are continuously downhill, our pace picked up. I had no thoughts during this early stage. I just moved, propelled by my commitment to honor my son but still lost in the grief that pressed my shoulders down so that my legs felt oh so heavy as I slogged along through Asheville and Framingham.

The thing about the Boston Marathon is that it really is two races, with the first half, as I said, being basically downhill and the second requiring a tremendous effort for every runner to bring it home.

The most famous part of the course, Heartbreak Hill, is actually a series of hills—five of them to be exact—that taxed the body nearly to the breaking point. If you've run too hard in those first twelve miles, your quads will be screaming as you work your way up Heartbreak Hill to the top, where you're greeted by the ladies of Wellesley College. It has been a tradition for over fifty years for these beautiful coeds to cheer every runner over the top of Heartbreak.

Races have been won and lost at this nineteen-mile juncture. Boston's Billy Rodgers broke the field on Heartbreak Hill. Both John Kelleys—unrelated marathoners with the same name—made their move right there on Heartbreak to win; and Clarence DeMar, the first great Boston Marathoner, always said that Heartbreak separated the men from the boys. And until women joined the event in the seventies, that really was the case.

So there we were, a minister and a blind man, trying to work our way up Heartbreak Hill.

There are moments in every marathon when runners—whether they are in the front of the pack or at the back—are all tested. Everyone is extended to the breaking point. Muscle fibers throb in pain. Breathing rasps its way from the lungs, burning the throat and chest.

It does not matter what level of runner you are—there will be a moment in every marathon when you have the feeling that it isn't worth it, that you might as well quit and walk in. I'm sure that's the case for all amateurs in these moments of physical and emotional stress, and only through intense human resolve do they find the strength to reach the top of Heartbreak Hill.

In the first eighteen miles of the race, Clayton and I were right on time with our eight-minute pace. Actually, we were about two minutes ahead of what we'd intended, but as we snaked our way up Heartbreak we slowed, and I found myself thinking, *Well, there goes three-thirty. We'll never run that time.*

In the distance I heard the cheering, loud and long, from the ladies of Wellesley and thought we were closer to the top than we really were.

"Take it easy," Clayton warned, through his heavy breathing. "I know you can hear them, but there's still two more parts to climb."

"Okay," I said, dropping my chin and digging in.

It is difficult enough to guide a blind person when you're running. It is many times more difficult when you're running a marathon and you're tired yourself. Exhaustion prompts the mind to wander and, I suppose, so does the sight of the lovely girls from Wellesley.

As we finally lifted ourselves over the top of Heartbreak Hill, for the first and only time Clayton missed a pothole in the road. In a second my right foot found it. My ankle turned over, and I went down in a heap. Runners scrambled to get around us without stomping me into the pavement. Clayton and two other good Samaritan athletes pulled me to the side of the road.

It's over, I thought. That was my consuming awareness as my ankle throbbed. *The marathon is over. I'm done.*

Clayton was kneeling next to me, and I knew he felt worse about my fall than I did.

"I'm sorry, Brian," he said. "I wasn't paying attention. Do you think you can go on?"

Before I could answer my friend, my mind began to play tricks on me. Was it fatigue? Pain? Delirium? Or was it a miracle? In that moment I was transformed from a person who had lived more than forty years blind to all the visuals of life to one who could see. Oh, I don't mean that I was looking at runners going by or a cloud formation or even my friend Clayton's face. No, my eyes were not externally taking in the world, but my mind's eye saw— in true living color—Tommy. He was dressed in his baseball uniform, and he was smiling at me.

"Hi, Dad," he said. "How you doing?"

I don't know if I answered him out loud or in my mind, but I said, "I guess I'm done, Tommy. This is the end of the marathon for me."

"No, it's not," Tommy said, sounding as if he was now my coach instead of my son. "We still have to get to Boston. Remember, Mom and Shannon are waiting for you there."

"But my ankle . . . "

"Oh, that's nothing," he said. "All you have to do is get up. I'll help you."

"On angel's wings?" I said, smiling.

"No," he said cheerfully. "I haven't got those. I'm just a guide."

"Like the Holy Spirit," I said.

I drew my legs under me and stood up, feeling as if Tommy's arms were under mine and he was lifting me, not with the strength of an eleven-year-old but with a power far beyond physical limits.

I was on my feet and smiling, actually laughing out loud.

"Come on, Clayton! Let's go. We can still make that three-thirty time."

"What are you talking about?" my friend said.

"I'm talking about"—I looked up—"I'm talking about Tommy. Right, Tommy?"

"Right, Dad," Tommy said. "Let's go."

As we ran, Tommy kept telling me how much he loved me and how I shouldn't worry about him, that he was happy in heaven, that it was everything the Bible said. No tears. No fears. No cancer. And on his spiritual wings we ate up the last 10K, forcing Clayton to run at maximum effort just to hang on. In fact, as we came off Beacon Street and rocketed our way down Commonwealth Avenue, Clayton actually held on to my arm, and as Tommy lifted me I lifted my friend.

Now Tommy had become my cheerleader. "Go, Dad. That's awesome. Stay light on your feet. Pick up your pace. Let's go, Dad. Run!"

And I did.

As we rounded the last curve into Copley Square at the twenty-sixth mile mark, the timer called out, "Three twenty-nine oh one."

"No!" Clayton said. "We're not going to make it."

"Oh, yes, we are," I said.

"Yes, we are," Tommy agreed.

I was sprinting now, like Clarence DeMar, the two John Kelleys, Bill Rodgers, Frank Shorter, Joan Benoit, and all the other world-class marathoners who had won this great race. I was now one of them—an elite runner—carried forward by something that was otherworldly.

I pulled Clayton toward the finish line, not letting him quit. He was remarkable, hanging on right to the end.

Forty yards from the finish line Tommy said, "I'm leaving you now, Dad."

"Why?" I said. "Why?"

"Because you need to finish this yourself."

"But Tommy—"

"Don't worry," he said. "I'll always be here."

"I love you," I said. "I love you." Tommy disappeared slowly from my mind's eye and I stretched the last few strides, crossing the finish line.

The timer said, "Three twenty-nine fifty-eight."

We had done it—Clayton McRae and I—bonded by our friendship and lifted by the love and grace of a little boy's spirit.

Bridgette and Shannon were right there at the end of the chutes, and as I hugged them, exhausted but ebullient, I told them over and over again that everything would be all right. Somehow we would make it as a family, Tommy would always be with us, and though he had lost his physical battle with cancer, his sweet spirit would keep us close until the day came when we would join him in the kingdom of heaven.

I don't think I actually used all of those words as I hugged my family, but what I do know—what I was sure of—was that at the end of twenty-six miles, three hundred and eight-five yards of the Boston Marathon I believed that I would never be without Tommy's presence, and I knew that somehow I would continue to grow in love—and yes, in faith.

epilogue

One year later

I often hear people say that after a tragedy occurs, they put the pieces of their lives back together. I don't think that's how it works. What happens is that you create a new life, and it's a life in which you restructure all of your priorities.

I'm learning to take great pleasure living with two women. I suppose I'm developing my sensitive side. Actually, what I think is happening is that I'm becoming a better communicator, probably because with Tommy's passing I've come to understand that every moment I'm given needs to be appreciated, especially the ones I spend with those I love.

I'm still a hard charger in the District Attorney's office, but I'm also much more involved in all of Shannon's activities than I ever was before. Shannon seems to be a little quieter and more intro-spective as she grows. I think she's sensitive about being our only child, so she works to involve us in all the things that interest her.

Bridgette surprised me. She joined the hospice group at Dana-Farber as a home skill nurse. And from everything I've heard from

Dr. Hennessy, she is tremendous at interacting with patients who are preparing to cross over from this life to the next.

And what about me? Well, I'm getting ready for the next Boston Marathon with my friend Rev. Clayton McRae. Last year we raised about $200,000 together in what I now call the Tommy Marathon, and this year we think we might even do better, although we joke about the fact that we probably won't run anywhere near three-thirty based on our training and the fact that I know Tommy's going to make me do this one completely on my own.

I don't want you to think that his sweet spirit is not still right there over my shoulder, and part of the lives of all the O'Connors. Whenever any of us feel depressed or sad and think about our ultimate loss, something always seems to happen that lifts our spirits. Now, I'm not saying that Tommy is manipulating our situation with some kind of heavenly intervention, but what I am sure of is that when we think of his character, his spirit, his enthusiasm, and his courage, we overcome our depression and continue to grow in love and purpose.

So maybe that's what the Holy Spirit does. Maybe the Holy Spirit invests us with God's hope for each of us that we, as His children, will continue to evolve in love and faith.

And what about faith? Well, Bridgette has remained a practicing Catholic, and we still attend Mass as a family. I can't say that I'm necessarily comfortable in the Church yet, but I do love the beauty of the sacraments and the majesty of the Mass.

If I had to define what's different for me in terms of God based on my conversations with Clayton and the significance of Tommy's life and death, it is that I have clearly embraced the one true and everlasting God. God is in me and with me, and I am now committed to that fundamental belief.

Let me try to express it this way: I live each day of my earthly life knowing that Tommy's spirit renews my faith and reminds me that someday, along with Bridgette and Shannon, I will once again embrace my son in the kingdom of heaven. I miss him, but I celebrate him—as Clayton said, Tommy's truly was a short life well lived.

Amen.

Reader's Guide Questions

1. Does Brian's blindness help him be a better parent? If so, how?

2. Does his marriage benefit from Brian's disability? If so, how?

3. Can you relate to Brian's struggle with faith? Have you ever questioned whether God was truly good? What was your conclusion?

4. What kind of pain do you think a sibling (i.e., Shannon) goes through when a brother or sister is very ill? How can a parent help?

5. Is the character of Clayton McRae realistic? What did you like/dislike about him?

6. What can we learn about the O'Connors' struggle with cancer that can help us with our own life tragedies?

7. Have you ever supported parents going through the same difficulties the O'Connors faced? What did you do for them?

8. What did you learn from Brian's struggle with faith?

9. How do you view God after reading this book?

10. Describe Tommy's faith through his ordeal. Is it a faith you'd like to emulate?